The Cartier Project

MIHA MAZZINI

The Cartier Project

TRANSLATED FROM THE SLOVENIAN
by Maja Visenjak-Limon

SCALA HOUSE PRESS

FIRST NORTH AMERICAN EDITION 2004
Text copyright ©1987 Miha Mazzini
Translation copyright ©2004 by Maja Visenjak-Limon

This is a work of fiction. Names, places, characters, and incidents are either products of the author's imagination or are used fictitiously.

ISBN: 0-9720287-4-9

Published in the United States by
Scala House Press
an imprint of

Scala House Publishers, LLC
PO Box 17964
Seattle, Washington 98107
www.scalahousepress.com

Printed in Canada

Library of Congress Cataloging-in-Publication Data

Mazzini, Miha.
  [Operacija Cartier. English]
  The Cartier Project / Miha Mazzini ; translated from the Slovenian
by Maja Visenjak-Limon.– 1st North American ed.
      p. cm.
  ISBN 0-9720287-4-9
  I. Visenjak-Limon, Maja. II. Title.
PG1919.23.A99O6813 2004
891.8'436–dc22
                          2004012513

INTRODUCTION

The most amazing fact about Tito's Yugoslavia was its lack of a singular, uniform identity: the country spread across a large part of the Balkans and was an incredible mixture of cultures, languages and religions (Orthodox, Muslim, Christian, communist—you name it). I grew up in the northern industrial town of Jesenice, a town that was considered to be a microcosm of sorts, a Yugoslavia in miniature: people from all over the country came to work in the town's foundries and brought with them their own brands of cultures and religions. Even when Tito died in 1980, it seemed as though that amazing coexistence would last.

Growing up, I noticed that some people in the human river that flooded the streets of the town to and from the factory three times a day were trying desperately to be different, but the models we had to choose from were limited. It was a small, isolated town, and films at the local cinema were the only real sources of "foreign" images we had access to: tough guys with golden chains around their necks; cowboys, both American and Mexican; and of course a few Indians in costumes seen in the East German westerns.

I suffered from such a lack of identity as a kid that my favorite comic book hero was *The Invisible Man*; that's probably why I always loved the movies where one of the characters, who is practically non-existent throughout most of the film, is revealed at the end to be a writer telling everybody how it really was and forcing us to realize that we were watching his story all that time.

My first thought, then, was to write a script, but I had to ask myself realistically who would want to film it. So I decided to write a novel instead; a prequel to a future script. I was working part time as a night watch where I had a lot of time to think about the story and characters, and I had an hour or two for typing during the days after I put my baby daughter to sleep. It seems to me today that a good part of *The Cartier Project* is typical male baby-sitting stuff — I was writing about the things I was without at the time (booze, sex, poetry readings...). The style of the writing was definitely borne out of baby-sitting circumstances: short sentences meant that I didn't have to press so many keys on the typewriter and make so much noise; short paragraphs because I had to constantly check if my daughter was still sleeping.

When *The Cartier Project* was published in 1987, it sold 54,000 copies in a language spoken by fewer than two million people. The novel won both the state and the opposition award for the best novel of the year and that was probably the only thing that both sides agreed upon in those late stages of the Yugoslavian disintegration. Unfortunately, after the book was published, inflation soared astronomically, queues for petrol formed, and the general state of the Yugoslavian economy took a dive. When I finally received my share of royalties from the publisher for the 54,000 sales, the money was only barely enough to buy a good (but not extravagant) dinner for my family and two friends. The fortune from my aspiring writing career would have to wait for better times.

As I was re-reading the novel before this publication, I

spent the first few chapters just sighing over how much better I could do with the story today. But after awhile I let go of my embarrassment and criticism, and the story hooked me once again. As it did for tens of thousands of readers at a time when all I had wanted to do was to write a prequel to a never-written and long-forgotten script and — without knowing it at the time — take the first of many steps in a long journey to find myself.

Miha Mazzini
Ljubljana, Slovenia
January, 2004

PART ONE

I don't wanna hear about what the rich are doing
I don't wanna go to where the rich are going
– Joe Strummer, The Clash, 1977

Whatever next.
– Ibro Hadžipuzić, The Foundry, 1983

CHAPTER 1

After three days of starvation, I gave in and took it from under the bed. The small, round, dented tin. The label said something about minced beef.

I didn't have the strength to look for the can opener. Dizziness came in waves. I took a hammer and a kitchen knife and made a hole in the lid. With the tip of the knife I scraped out the contents and gulped them down like a wild animal. I picked bits of tobacco from the seams of my pockets, added the leftovers from the ashtray, and rolled a cigarette with a scrap of newspaper.

There was a mouthful of liquid left in the bottle on the windowsill. I gulped it down.

My stomach rejected the stale, lukewarm beer, which had been scorched by the sun. I barely managed to get to the bathroom and stick my head down the toilet. With a sad look, I said goodbye to the fragments of meat, stood on my tiptoes, and pulled the string on the cistern. There were only a few centimeters of water left. I took a cold shower. There was no hot water. Bare wires stuck out of the wall where the water heater should have been.

I put on clean underwear and socks. I immediately washed the dirty ones with soap and hung them over the window to dry for the next day. I put on my combat jacket and jeans again. And tennis shoes. I nearly fainted when I bent over to tie the laces.

The lace tore in my hand. I couldn't prolong its life. There was no room. Knot after knot.

I took the piece of string from the toilet cistern and tied my tennis shoes. I straightened up and looked in the mirror. I waited for the fog in my eyes to clear.

The Cartier bottle was empty.

I was devastated. Even though I'd always known it would happen sooner or later. I was left without the one thing I could not do without.

I turned the bottle upside down, put a finger under it, and waited.

It fell.

The last drop of perfume.

I dabbed it on my neck.

I put the top on the bottle and stood it upside down. Maybe more would come. I went out onto the street. Everything was gray. No color anywhere.

This always happens to me after three sleepless nights. I leaned against the wall and waited. The picture was moving and splitting in two, sometimes drowning in fog. A woman marched past. Her sweater suddenly became bright red. The contrast hurt my brain. Soon after, the color came back, first to the sky, then to the smoke, and finally the houses took on a reddish tint. The dusty pavement was streaked with streams and puddles left by the melting snow. The foundry fence ran along to my right.

The bar was empty. The waitress was sitting behind the counter drinking coffee and reading a trashy novel. She glanced at me. Then immediately carried on reading the book.

Written by me.

I sat at the table in the corner, made a pillow with my arms, and fell asleep. When I woke up, the first thing I noticed was a different body behind the counter. The book was lying by the till. It was dark outside. I looked around the room, searching for victims. At the next table there were some pensioners drinking spritzers. Next to the exit, a tall, muscular guy in a long-sleeved T-shirt and jeans was slowly sipping beer from a glass.

On his T-shirt there was a coat of arms and underneath it said "UCLA."

That's supposed to mean the University of California Los Angeles, wherever that is. I bet he'd never been there. He probably hadn't even been to the primary school in Lower Bottomley. A worker at the foundry, an immigrant from the south. He came to the bar every night for a beer. When the waitress started putting the chairs on the tables, he would get up and leave. No hassle, no drunken singing, he would never even talk to anybody.

I didn't have enough strength in me for breaking new ground, I preferred to concentrate on my eyes, which were blurring and seeing double. I managed to control them somehow and concentrated on the table at the other end of the room, where a woman I didn't know was sitting with two vultures of my sort, Hippy and Poet. In front of them were half-empty bottles of beer. No doubt the woman had paid for them and, in doing so, bought the unconditional support of both parasites.

There was nothing left to do but join them. I pulled myself together, focused on a spot on Poet's bald patch, pushed my chair back, and rushed to their table before dizziness knocked me over. I grabbed a chair and sat down. I adjusted the image in front of my eyes and caught a surprised expression on the woman's face and quite friendly looks from Hippy and Poet, as if they didn't mind me muscling in on the act. The woman must have been loaded. All three of us would be able to drink on her all evening.

"What's up with you?" she asked. I looked her in the eyes. I didn't like her. She gave the impression of being bloated — no, inflated.

"I'd like a beer."

I got it.

I could feel the icy liquid slide down my throat. Then splash against the walls of my stomach. I could barely stop myself from throwing up and fell to sipping it slowly.

The woman talked and talked. Instead of words, balloons were coming from her mouth.

She said, "Blablabla."

Hippy said, "Transcendence."

Poet said, "Poetry."

A new round.

Her again. "Blablabla."

And so on. Endlessly. All together, "Blablablatranscendenceblablablapoetryblablablanirvanablablablablablabla . . ."

They were dancing in circles. Hippy and Poet, high on the free booze, would have agreed with the devil himself. She, quite a bit younger than the rest of us, was drunk from the status she'd managed to buy for herself. She wasn't used to having money. Some cash had come her way from somewhere. Maybe she'd stolen it. It didn't matter. There'd be none left by tomorrow.

She was enjoying her new role. We were nodding like toy dogs.

Suddenly I felt disgusted with it all. I was drunk after one glass. A result of my three-day fast.

There's no difference between selling yourself for a drink and selling yourself on the street. Both are simple whoring. I tried to collect myself and follow the conversation.

"I've never seen such a shitty film."

"It just wasn't contemplative."

"Or poetic," added the other echo.

Her again. "A crap film."

The echoes didn't add anything meaningful to her conclusions.

"He hasn't got a clue, that Polanski." She started another round.

They were talking about the film *Tess*.

I pushed my chin forward. Made room in my mouth for my voice to sound deeper. I like bass.

"You have no idea, do you?" I blurted out so aggressively that she turned towards me. Up until then, she had barely noticed me. I'd been on the outer edge of her charity circle.

Hippy and Poet looked at me with horror. They thought I must have gone mad. Throwing away free booze. They looked at me as if I'd just appeared from Mars. She lifted her head and struck back.

"You know, I can do my own thinking. I don't have to agree with you."

A game of poker was just beginning. Time to bluff.

I leaned forward, almost into her face. She stared back at me stubbornly.

"Don't you think," I said, "that the scene where the heroine, on becoming the owner of the plantation, gathers together all the black slaves and gives them their freedom, is a hymn to humanity?"

She couldn't compete.

"Well . . . of course . . ."

Her voice lost its confidence. Silence would have meant surrender. She had to say something.

"I liked that, too, that scene. Before, I was talking about the overall impression the film had on me."

I fell back in my chair. I almost hugged myself with satisfaction. He who bluffs, wins. All that remained was a routine which had to be carried out as speedily and forcefully as possible.

"Which film were you talking about, my dear?"

"*Tess*."

"You're not going to believe this." I looked her in the eyes with feigned confusion and surprise. "There were no black slaves in that film and no bullshit about freeing them."

Embarrassment. Pure, naked embarrassment.

I left her to fall apart for a few seconds in silence. Then said in a by-the-way sort of way, "So you're criticizing something you haven't even seen?"

"I have."

"You haven't."

"Have."

"Haven't."

Faster and faster. Blow after blow. Every word a direct hit. Right next to her face. Her breath smelled sour.

Finally she gave in.

"I read a review in the paper."

"How can you talk about thinking for yourself, then?"

She floundered.

"I read this critic's reviews regularly and I know we always agree."

Leaned back in my chair. Talking calmly and contentedly.

"So you should have said earlier, 'We can think for ourselves.'"

Finally she got it. Who was I to interrogate and humiliate her at her expense? She got up, saying she had to catch a bus.

Hippy and Poet looked at me with unconcealed hatred. They immediately offered to see her to the bus stop. She gracefully accepted their offer.

I didn't force myself on them.

They left.

I felt exhausted and content, as if I had just graduated in cross-examination at the MI5, CIA, and KGB and became a correspondent member of a few other similar organizations around the world. I took a last sip from the bottle and let it slip slowly down my throat.

Any further ones I had kissed goodbye.

"Oh well," I sighed weakly when I felt the waitress approaching from behind me, probably to collect the empty bottle. I didn't lift my gaze from its green glass. A hand with garishly painted nails grabbed the bottle and took it away.

And put a new one in its place.

I looked up so quickly that my jaw couldn't keep up and stayed open. A frame for a dumb look. The waitress, as if she couldn't believe it either, gestured to the table behind my back.

The guy with the UCLA logo nodded to me.

Undoubtedly an invitation. Feeling unsociable, I preferred to stay where I was and turned towards the door.

Hippy and Poet were now drinking and nodding in another bar. I was separated from them only by one of my occasional attacks of aggression or, as I called it, character. It probably wouldn't last much longer. Certainly not as long as Hippy's thirty, or Poet's forty, years. At twenty-two there's nothing to decide anymore. You've got to decide during puberty. Between death and growing old. After that, everything else is self-delusion.

With an occasional kick from the spirit which can't quite reconcile itself to reality.

Hippy was a remnant of 1968, like many others in our villages and remote hills. He rolled joints, talked about transcendence, occasionally cut an inch off his shoulder-length hair, sticky with grease. If he became too engrossed during smoking, he would sometimes burn his beard and look a couple of years younger. He bummed for bread and drink, which Poet, on the other hand, didn't need to do at all. He worked at the foundry every morning, had his lunch there, too. In the afternoon he only drank on somebody else's account. He never used a penny of his salary. Everything went to his self-publishing ventures. He published a volume of his poetry every two months. A day or two after publication, in a navy-blue suit with a carefully brushed artist's beard, he'd be selling samples in the bar. His total number of customers in a year was smaller than the number of his fingers. After two days of persistence he would disappointedly admit defeat. Once again, he would put on his scruffy brown jacket and his brown trousers with the small flowery pattern, get drunk, and hand out the leftover copies of his work of art to anybody who cared to reach for them. There must have been seventy of his books in my flat. I'd read two of them and sworn never to open another. I kept my word, but that is not a proof of my strong character. Resisting such a small temptation is no great virtue.

He'd had it best a few years ago when he'd gotten a job as a primary school magazine editor. He resigned from the foundry immediately and dedicated himself right away to collecting articles from the hopeful young literati. The school had its own committee of children who sorted, cut, and bound the sheets. A printing house offered to print the front and back cover for nothing to help the aspiring artists.

That year, twenty-two new volumes of poetry were published by our Poet and one reduced issue of the school magazine due, according to Poet's editorial, to technical problems and lack of material. After he was kicked out, he went back to his job at the foundry.

This bottle, too, was empty. It was time to talk to the UCLA guy. I moved seats. He immediately waved to the waitress and held up two fingers.

That, of course, meant two more beers. I started to like him. His appearance was different from the other immigrant workers at the foundry. He was wearing tennis shoes, not the winkle-pickers with raised heels everyone else was wearing. His jeans were the right length and not turned up on the inside. His hair was closely cropped and he had a few days growth of stubble. He even had the kind of nose and lips you'd expect. There was something in his eyes which confused me for a moment. As if I had already seen them somewhere before. Not the eyes themselves, probably just the look. I couldn't remember where and when.

He said, "I'm Selim."

He hesitated a moment before offering me his hand.

"Egon."

He nodded as if he already knew my name.

"I liked the film, too."

I was surprised at his pronunciation. He couldn't have been in this town long. I'd been seeing him in the bar for only about two years. He spoke almost without an accent.

"Yeah, yeah." I nodded and decided not to tell him that I hadn't seen the film at all. I'd only read Hardy's novel.

The waitress brought the two beers.

I stared at the table, which was scratched and carved by knives. We avoided familiarities, such as toasts and knocking glass against glass. He didn't try anything like that.

I took a gulp. Selim was talking about the film. I couldn't follow. Drunkenness hit me on the back of the skull with its full power. Images split into four and scattered. I was trying to catch hold of the space, to patch it together. Gave up in the end. I was looking at the face in front of me, which was distorted and mangled as in a fairground hall of mirrors.

"The film was beautiful."

He breathed the word "beautiful" so gently.

The waitress started turning chairs upside down and putting them on the tables.

"TIME TO GOOOOOOO!" I heard just behind my ear.

And we went. The last two. We stopped in the street. He looked at me questioningly, as if to say, "Let's go to another bar." I stumbled. In the foundry, which was filling all of my visual field, they opened a furnace and the night became red.

I was interested to see whether a goodbye or vomit would come out if I opened my mouth.

I managed to speak.

"See you around. Cheers!"

"Cheers."

I ran into the narrow passage behind the bar. Leaned my head against the wall and left my signature on it. Took a few steps away from the sour liquid. Sat down and had a nap. I was woken by repeated stomach spasms, which pushed the rest of the drink out into the open and choked me for a while longer. It passed. Leaning on the wall, I took pleasure in the view, which became crystal clear. I was observing a thin trickle of saliva dangling from my lip, lit by the flames leaping from the top of the chimney.

I took a few trial steps and, happy with the result, went off to Karla's.

The road by the foundry was completely empty. The well-behaved workers went to bed with the cows. The less well be-haved took to singing maudlin love songs in the bar. The howl-ing voices of the singers accompanied me as I walked.

Karla lived on the third floor. I listened tactfully with my ear to the door. All I could hear was the radio. A woman's voice was reading the news from around the world, wherever that may be.

No fuck-inducing record on the stereo. Okay. I rang the bell. Karla opened the door wrapped in a man's orange bath-robe. She'd just had a bath. Fresh. Sweet smelling.

I peeked inside the flat, just in case. She shook her head and asked, "Hungry?"

"Yeah."

I received her most beautiful smile, which always drove me wild. An uncovered row of upper teeth. One tooth always slightly biting the bottom lip.

"Come in, I've got some soup left over from lunch."

I took off my shoes. My toes peeped out of my socks to greet Karla. I put on the slippers that she offered me and fol-lowed her to the kitchen.

She turned off the radio. Somewhere in the building a man and a woman were arguing. A child was screaming. The usual urban silence. Karla had her washed hair wrapped in a white towel, turban-like. She lit the gas with a match and put on the pan. She leaned on the kitchen counter and watched me sit at the table. Above me a light, not too strong, with a paper shade.

"Another study attack?"

I shrugged my shoulders. I admitted. What else could I do.

"Whose turn was it this time?"

"Thomas Aquinas."

She laughed.

"And how long did it last?"

"Three days and two nights."

"Then you really do need a bowl of hot soup."

I wasn't in the habit of coming to Karla for food. Only after my occasional studious attacks, as she called them, I showed up at her place to eat. Ate the leftovers from lunch, or an egg.

"You won't believe me, but I can just picture you. Bent over a book for three days and two nights. Your only movement the turning of a page. When is it enough for you? When you faint?"

"Yeah, that's about right."

She poured the contents of the pan into a china bowl. Usually we would drink tea out of it. She set the table for me, gave me a spoon, and sat down opposite me.

The light shone on the little creases which had developed at the corners of her mouth and eyes.

"Egon, you're not getting religious, are you? Weren't you studying *De Civitate Dei* last time?"

Her voice had a throaty, velvety quality. I always thought of it when somebody mentioned Berlin in the thirties. A whore's voice.

"No, that was the one before."

"And the last one?"

"The phone book."

Laughter.

"That's exactly what I like about you most. Your unpredictability is so predictable. Like the time when you had that punk group, what were you, The Young Komsomols, or something like that?"

She shut up. We had a quiet, gentlemanly agreement that we did not talk about each other's pasts, in any shape or form. Sometimes one of us slipped. She more often than me. She was getting old. I had seven years' advantage.

She immediately changed subjects.

"Do you want some more?"

She pointed to the empty bowl.

"No."

I stretched my hand and caught her earlobe between my second and middle fingers. She leaned her head on my palm and rubbed against my hand like a cat. I stroked her with my fingers from her temples to her chin. Gently, only barely touching her with my fingertips. Just a warming-up touch. The skin of every woman is different to the touch and has a different scent. You can sense the scent unique to each woman in spite of perfumes or deodorants.

I moved to the chair next to her.

I traced the path of the fingers with my slightly open lips. I filled my nostrils with Karla's scent. With my tongue wandering around her face, I found her tongue and started to tease it.

She moved away and said, "You're always in need of something. When you're no longer hungry, you get horny."

There was a trace of mockery in her eyes.

With my left hand I slowly, slowly slid into the opening of her robe. Pulled it open a bit further. A small, nicely formed breast peeped out. I circled it with my fingers. My index finger traced where her breast joined her body. I bent over and repeated the movement with my tongue. I found the nipple and licked it slowly, teased it out into the open. I kissed the erect nipple and moved to the other one. Karla pressed herself against me, ruffling my hair. Her tongue drilled into my ear.

An alarm clock went off.

For the second time that day, I managed to put on a really moronic look.

And an upward one at that, which doesn't happen very often because of my height.

"It's time for you to leave." She whispered, breathing deeply, she was sorry. This, too, was a part of our agreement.

I got up. Went to the door. She arranged her robe and saw me to the front door. In the doorway to the corridor, I turned around. We embraced and kissed. Nothing refined, just pure lust. Our bodies nearly crushed.

Gently, but decisively, she pushed me away.

A look into my eyes.

I nodded.

I bent over for my shoes when she said, "You can leave your socks here, before they fall completely apart, and the jacket, too. The collar is in shreds."

Blows always come from above. A third idiotic look. I surpassed my yearly norm. If there's anything unimaginable in this world, it's Karla darning socks.

She laughed.

"No, not me. I'm expecting a visit from on older, respectable gentleman, who very much likes doing a few chores. It relaxes him, he says."

"Okay."

If that's the case, that's all right. I took off my socks, put the tennis shoes on my bare feet, and gave her my jacket. I checked the pockets first and divided the small objects I always have on me between the pockets in my trousers.

"You can get them tomorrow morning. But don't wake me up. I'll leave them in a bag in the cupboard in the corridor."

She opened the door to show me where.

I hesitated. Tried to hug her once more. She moved away,

and suddenly I found myself outside the door. Every woman should master the basic toreador skills.

"Karla . . ."

"Yes?"

"Bye."

There was no point.

She said goodbye and her eyes sadly followed me. Or maybe I just imagined it. The wood was like all wood on doors. A ray of light was shining through the peephole, which wasn't darkened by an eye. I felt my way through the dark to the light switch, turned on the light, and left.

My stomach, full of soup, helped me nicely to stay upright.

I stopped at the fence that separates the foundry from the workers' dormitories.

The furnaces were humming, and somewhere gas was hissing. From the foundry's darkness, three workers in blue overalls came running out and climbed over the fence about three meters away from me. When the last one reached the ground, I shouted, "Hey, you!"

He practically shat himself. Security! A guard! He'd been caught! Panic!

The other two had already disappeared into the dark.

"Give me a cig."

He turned, full of pure relief. He pushed a half-full cigarette packet into my hand and ran after his friends.

You have to pick the right psychological moment for bumming.

I smoked a cigarette, leaning on the fence. Taking pleasure in the dizziness smoking causes after abstinence.

I started to feel cold. Early spring isn't the most suitable time to take a walk wearing just a T-shirt. A guard dressed in a gray uniform appeared inside the fence. He approached me quietly, thinking I was one of his flock that had gone astray. I turned around and grinned at him. He looked away and continued walking along the fence, suspiciously looking back over the clip on his shoulder every few steps. Workers who had lost an arm or a leg — accident survivors — become guards and wait for retirement. There's never a shortage of them. Every day new ones become qualified. God knows how many bones there are inside this fence. I spat at the wire mesh and went on.

I felt a terrible weariness. A quiet sadness. The only thing I really liked in this fucked-up settlement was walking in the middle of the night through the deserted streets covered with reddish foundry dust that sticks to the soles of your shoes.

In front of the cinema the woman ticket-seller was changing the poster and the photographs in the display case before she went home. She needed to talk so much that she could barely wait for me to come near enough. The glass on the front of the case was broken. I had to avoid the fragments scattered on the ground.

"Vandals, they're just vandals," she said. The neon light was still intact and it was on. The woman's face was shining like wax in the pale glow. The last film she'd watched was probably from the time when Esther Williams appeared in *Bathing Beauty*. After that, she couldn't watch any others because she had to sell tickets to the latecomers and for later performances. She was old, with backcombed hair. The sort of hairstyle you don't often see now. Her brightly colored lips were shining at me. The lipstick had been applied so thickly it leveled the wrinkles around her mouth and the lips appeared stuck on. Mistakenly brought from somewhere else, from another woman. From another time.

"Why do they have to break the glass if they want a poster? They should just come to me and I'd give them one for free. Have you any idea how much such a large pane of glass costs?"

I didn't make any effort to reply. She'd tell me eventually. The case was empty. The green cover on the back was full of holes from the tacks.

The woman told me the price. The amount hit me on the back as I was leaving. It really was quite high.

I locked the door behind me, sat on the only chair, and lit a cigarette. I smoked slowly in the dark room. From time to time the light of the flame from the chimney lit up the walls, but it still couldn't remove Karla from my eyes.

I threw the cigarette butt into the empty beer can and sighed. I undid my trousers, took my prick in my hand, and slowly, sadly jerked myself off, thinking of Karla. I sighed once more, had a shower, and went to bed.

I think Bukowski would have been very pleased with these last few sentences.

CHAPTER 2

The block of flats where Karla lived was unusually quiet at this time. Everybody was at work. Children at nurseries. Karla was asleep. I put my ear to the door, but I couldn't hear anything. In the cupboard, there was a white plastic bag with my socks and jacket, both mended. I kept turning the socks over in my hand, admiring the precise and perfect handiwork. The collar on the jacket was sewn on and hemmed with a special kind of seam that would stop it from coming undone again. I couldn't make out where the thread went. I'd never seen anything like it. I was roused from my admiration by sudden darkness. I didn't try to feel for the light switch. Putting one foot in front of the other, feeling for the stairs, I made it to the exit. Just inside the main entrance, I put on the socks by the light coming through the pane of thick, reinforced glass in the middle of the door.

I set off past the foundry with a purpose.

A group of workers hanging about inside came running up to the fence.

"Hey you, come here."

They were gesturing with their hands, inviting me over. I went.

"What do you want?"

"A liter of whisky," said the first one and pushed a bank note through the mesh of the fence. I took the money and went to the next one.

"A liter of wine."

"Schnapps."

"Brandy."

"A liter of red."

I took the money and quietly repeated the orders.

There was a whole line of them by the fence now. They were all pushing their hands through the fence. Like a field of wheat, all waving notes.

The money, crumpled, dirty, rolled into little balls, filled both my hands. My memory capacity was full, too.

"That's enough," I said to the next one.

"Don't be a cunt, get mine, too."

"And how do you think I'll carry it all? I've only got two hands."

"Go on, just mine."

I turned around and marched to the shop.

I was followed by a hail of curses.

I bought what I could remember. I snuck two bottles of wine in the bag while the sales assistant went to the back store-room for the schnapps. I paid and returned to the fence. There was nobody to be seen. A guard was disappearing behind a building.

As soon as I put the bags down, the men appeared from behind the containers, the rolls of wire, and the scrap metal, and rushed towards me.

We removed pieces of turf from under the fence. I slid the bottles down a small tunnel, dug some time ago and just large enough for a bottle. Hands on the other side grabbed the booze. The men disappeared in a flash. I leaned on the fence post and counted the profits. The agreed ten percent, plus the two stolen bottles, plus some change from the ones who hadn't given me the exact amount — I have a policy of not giving change — not bad at all. I could sense the guard creeping up on me from behind. This time it was somebody with a wooden leg. I looked back at him and grinned, showing all my teeth.

While I can still move, you can't get to me.

I put the money in my pocket. The guard carried on with his eternal round.

Out of sheer bloody-mindedness I shouted as loud as I could, "See you tomorrow, lads!"

Before I went I grinned at the guard again, who was staring at me furiously.

My stomach rumbled, and I set off for Magda's.

I'd recently been going to her just to fuck and eat, to be honest. And even that not in a relaxed, happily parasitic mood, but with a feeling of guilt and uneasiness because I thought she really loved me. It wasn't really fair to her, and I'd stopped ringing at her door a few months ago. She later found me at the bar and started crying. There has to be a right time even for a kick in the ass.

Magda was a college schoolgirl. After school she'd cook lunch for her parents, who didn't return from the foundry until late afternoon.

She opened the door wearing jeans and a linen shirt which bulged with her large pear-shaped breasts.

We kissed.

"Did you run out of your perfume?"

We went into the kitchen with our arms around each other.

"That's right, there's no more Cartier."

"Are you ever going to tell me where you get the money for a new bottle? It can't be that cheap."

A glance at the stove and a sniff told me that nothing at all was cooking today. There was no sign that there would be either.

"Let's just say I have my sources. You know all great men have their little secrets."

We embraced and kissed.

Magda was the most quickly aroused of all the women I knew. Sometimes it seemed to me that her whole body was one large erogenous zone.

She moved away and looked at her watch.

"We don't have time, Egon. My parents are coming from work earlier today. It's my father's birthday, and I have to make him a cream cake."

"I'll help you."

She looked at me gratefully.

"Really?"

"If I say so, I will. Tell me what to do."

"I don't have to cook lunch. Father is taking us out to eat. Just help me with the cake."

She opened the fridge. Cartons of cream from top to bottom.

"Whip it with the electric mixer while I get the filling ready and chop up the fruit."

She brought the mixer and put it on the table.

I took the cartons from the fridge, one after another, took off the tops, and poured the contents into a bowl. I turned on the machine. While beating the cream, I amused myself by watching the rhythmic movement of Magda's breasts as she chopped the bananas, apricots, and apples.

"And where shall I put the whipped cream?"

She brought me a huge basin, almost as big as a bucket.

I shook the cream into it. Got the next three cartons, turned on the mixer, watched Magda's breasts. Got a hard-on.

The procedure went on and on. The basin was nearly full. A heap of chopped fruit was waiting on the table. Magda was busy with the filling. My prick was still hard.

There were four cartons left in the fridge.

I thought I should first do just three, which was the bowl's capacity, but I was so fed up I decided to do all four at once.

The bowl was filled up to the edge. A few drops spilled over. I switched on the mixer, and the cream splashed all over the kitchen. It ran down Magda's neck and back.

She trembled as the coldness touched her skin.

"Whoops, a mistake. A technical hitch. Don't panic, I'll soon have you clean."

I licked the cream from her ear and the tiny hairs on her neck.

She trembled.

I slowly unbuttoned her shirt and caught the drops of cream which were running down her back.

"No, Egon . . . please. I'm in such a hurry," she breathed pleadingly. I went back to the mixer, which was still on. I reached into the basin, took a handful, threw it at Magda, and switched off the machine.

"It splashed again, the bastard," I explained apologetically and dutifully licked the cream off her.

She firmly gripped the table.

She started breathing deeply and slowly turned towards me. I reached for the basin with both hands wanting to get another load, but lost balance and knocked it over so that the contents spilled out in heaps. I pulled Magda to the floor. We rolled in the cream. I penetrated her swiftly. We came together.

When she recovered, she started crying. She was on the verge of panic.

"My parents will be home in half an hour. And where's the cake?"

I burped. That made her even madder. I couldn't stop myself. My stomach was full of cream.

"What are we going to do?" She was desperate. She was sitting naked in the cream and moaning.

"Oh, ooooh, oooooooooh!"

Without stopping.

It was time for my organizational skills to manifest themselves.

"Calm down, it'll be all right."

She didn't seem to hear me.

"Hey, listen." I shook her by the shoulders. "Everything's going to be fine, half an hour is a lot of time, just help me."

I started scraping up the cream from the floor and putting it back in the basin. Magda sat and moaned for a while longer before joining me.

We set to work. We had no other option. I quickly picked the worst of the hairs and fluff out of the cream. We combined the fruit and the filling. I put the chocolate powder into a plastic bag, bit a corner off and shaped a message on the cake. She put the cake in the fridge. We dressed quickly.

Steps could be heard coming up the stairs. The door opened.

"So the test is on Monday?" I asked in a loud voice.

She immediately caught on.

"Yes, the last three lessons."

"Well, at least now I'll know what to revise."

"Good morning," I greeted her parents politely.

Her father looked at me suspiciously.

She explained that I was a fellow pupil who'd been ill all week. Her father must have been thinking I was repeating a year.

I politely said goodbye and left.

I belched again in the corridor. All that cream. A Laurel and Hardy porn show.

The sky was completely blue and spring was in the air. I was tempted to leave. To wherever.

Magda reminded me of the empty Cartier bottle. Soon I had to start thinking about how to get the money for a new one. At home I had another manuscript, finished a month ago.

A new trashy novel. Today might be the day to go and sell

it. I'd have to go up to the city and extract the money I was still owed. I could only dream of an advance.

After a relaxed train journey — I had to get off only three times, run to the other end of the train, and jump back on in order to avoid the ticket inspector — I arrived at the city. While waiting for a few minutes of the editor's time, slumped in a comfortable armchair, I smoked two cigarettes under the secretary's surreptitious glances. The editor was an eminent poet of high culture, working part time for the publisher of cheap paperbacks. Not under his real name, of course, but under a pseudonym. I published my shit under a female English name. That's what the majority of eminent writers and poets did; they had to earn a living somehow. They sent in their contributions by post. Nobody likes being caught in the act. I, too, had never told anybody about the source of my more or less regular income.

At last the secretary did me the honor of opening the door.

The editor pretended to be writing something. When I asked him when I'd get the money for *Pink Moonlight in the Bahamas*, he started fumbling through the ring binders. He phoned the secretary, who also started fumbling through the ring binders, before phoning someone else, who started . . .

And so on.

I smoked another two cigarettes.

I had just begun thinking about a third one when the phone rang. The editor listened to the outcome of the investigation. He smiled at me encouragingly: the payment request was already being processed.

"Great. I'll get it in six months then."

"Well, we'll see what we can do."

I don't often lose my temper, but when I do, I lose it so well that it's hard for me to find it again.

He listened to my yelling like Jesus listening to Pilate's judgment.

He didn't give a shit. After all, he was one of the chosen ones.

Yelling is most pleasurable when you're absolutely certain about the futility of your action.

He kept looking at his watch. A Seiko with a gold strap. Seiko means success in Japanese. He really had achieved that.

I stopped. I pulled my manuscript out of the envelope I'd been clutching under my arm and threw it on the desk.

"Will you at least publish this as soon as possible. Then I'll get two payments close together."

He opened the manuscript.

"*Naked and Barefoot*? Isn't the title a bit too provocative?"

"Either that or nothing," I snarled and marched off. The secretary couldn't be bothered to look up from the ring binders.

"Bye," she sang.

If you can't say goodbye, it's best not to say anything.

In the street again. Walking slowly to the old part of town.

I couldn't get rid of the feeling that the editor was going to throw a knife in my back. I could already feel a burning pain between my shoulder blades. Maybe they'd just lose that payment request in accounts. It'd take at least half a year to arrange a new one. It didn't really matter. But I still didn't have any Cartier. I'd have to finance it some other way. I walked into every bar. Looked around to find somebody who'd be so pleased to see me they'd buy me a drink. After maybe five bars or so I saw Alfred, my fellow townsman, sitting at an empty table. I joined him more out of tiredness than in the hope of a drink.

Alfred greeted me politely, as always. It was some kind of religious holiday, and he'd come to the city to attend Mass at the cathedral. He had all these holidays hierarchically listed. Every day was a small holiday and he attended Mass at a church near his flat. On Sundays, he went to the main church in town. For the bigger religious holidays he went to the cathedral in the capital. He planned to get married in St. Peter's in Rome, wherever that may be.

We chatted a bit. About things in general. About the weather. He didn't start talking about religion. I was probably the only person with whom he never discussed that. With everyone else he would roll his eyes and, faithful to the missionary spirit in him, paint a picture of salvation through faith. He'd tried it on me once, years before. Just once and never again.

Maybe because I could see that he was interested in other things besides life after death. After all, we had grown up together.

He was sipping his beer and choosing his words very carefully.

I didn't stray from the usual narrow course of our conversation by asking him for a drink.

He'd never offer to buy me one without being asked. Maybe, if I was lucky, he'd give me a sponge soaked in vinegar.

I soon said goodbye and left.

Another two bars, also without any success.

Where are you all, girls? Lost in the big city?

In the fourth bar, I finally got my beer. An acquaintance from the same town was pleased to see me. I pretended to be happier than was necessary out of embarrassment because I had forgotten his name. He still remembered mine. He was supposedly a poet. Or so I thought, because he invited me to that evening's literary gathering at the local public library where he'd be reading his poems together with some other poets. I promised to come. It was supposed to start at nightfall. I had another hour and a half till then. The acquaintance soon left, saying he had to go home to get his poems. He left enough money for both his and my beer.

I slowly emptied the bottle. It'd been a long time since I'd been to a literary evening, so my disgust with them had subsided a bit. Faded with memory. Quite perversely, I wanted to see the usual faces who gather at such meetings again. The waitress came to collect the two empty bottles. I offered her the money.

"Here, this is for the beer I've had and for another."

"And what about the one your friend had? Who'll pay for that?"

"Him? Didn't he pay?"

"No."

Her voice started to sound angry.

"He'll pay next time."

"Forget next time. You know him. You pay."

"What's the matter with you, which friend? I saw an empty seat, so I sat next to the guy. We spoke a few polite words. About the weather. Then he left. I've never seen him before."

I listened to the noises coming from the street. The noise of cars, voices, there was no cockerel crowing. I argued with the waitress a bit longer before she gave in and, muttering something to herself, brought me another beer.

"He must have forgotten to pay. Out of absentmindedness. Does he come in often?" I asked her reassuringly.

"Yes, often," she mumbled and left.

That's why she gave in so quickly. She was going to charge him next time.

And I wouldn't see him for at least another hundred years. And the forces of forgetfulness are strong. But as I didn't want to owe anybody anything, I was going to applaud him loudly for his poems.

Is there nothing more to life than selling yourself?

Thinking of prostitution, I thought of Karla.

Ooooh, Karla!

A wave of sadness swept over me.

Maybe I should start writing poems, too.

And Poet and I would publish together. We'd put on weight and nourish our bald patches together, arm-in-arm we would sigh about all the kindred spirits nobody understands. We'd work together at the foundry, watched by the guards, we'd buy drinks through the fence. From the younger generations who are only just arriving. Once you sit down, you stay seated.

You're dead.

I went to the bathroom to take a piss. When I saw that the floor wasn't flooded and that there was even toilet paper and soap, I decided to take a shit as well. Nothing but diarrhea came out. That damn cream.

As a child I loved *Gulliver's Travels*. The only children's book where the hero shits and pisses. And even that book hadn't really been written for children. It just never happens to anybody else. Because you can't live without doing it, you get a feeling that you're different. A dirt complex.

I returned to the table and finished my beer. Darkness was falling outside.

I went towards the exit and smiled at the waitress encouragingly. She didn't respond.

On the way to the library I lingered, looking at the shop windows. I even wanted to go into a bookstore and browse around, but I managed to stop myself. You've got to think of your reputation. And besides, the next day was Sunday, the day for my regular visit to the National Library. I hung around a bit longer outside the entrance where the literary evening was to happen. I didn't want to be too early, even though there's a strange sort of paradox in operation here. You're always too early coming to a literary event.

The room was already crammed with people, gathered in little groups. An enormous number of words were being spoken. The reading hadn't started yet. As I didn't belong to any of the cliques, I installed myself in a corner, sat on the windowsill, and lit a cigarette.

There were three cigarettes left. The smoke coming from my lungs joined the dense cloud all around the room. There were even some unknown faces.

The years since my last visit had taken their toll. There were some missing. They had probably got jobs as editors of cheap paperbacks, or they had hung themselves, or cut their wrists. That's the way the story goes.

Among the individuals I didn't recognize, a bony woman with a bob, wearing a long dress, made in India of course, attracted my attention the most.

I decided I'd fuck one of the poets of the younger generation tonight.

The expression "a poet of the younger generation" meant that the person was at least thirty years old. The one I was looking at wasn't any younger than that either. Her face wasn't beautiful, but it kept my interest until the beginning of the performance when all the participants piled into the hall. Sat down on the chairs arranged in rows. Closed the door behind them.

I didn't follow them straight away. It'd be a shame to waste a third of a cigarette. The acquaintance who'd earlier bought me a beer — well, two really — came hurrying by. He waved to me. I nodded to him and went in with him. I deliberately didn't sit next to him.

At the table in front of a wall, with two lights directed at him, with the rest of us in semi-darkness, somebody was already whining.

The hall was respectfully silent. People even tried to muffle their coughs in spite of the spring being the ideal time for colds. Then we clapped a bit, and somebody else came to sit at the table.

The first one returned to his seat.

The second one started whining.

Again, we clapped.

And the next one whined.

We all applauded, even the two who'd already done their whining. With horror, I realized that they were all going to do it. One after another, in the same order as they were sitting. There were only twenty-two in front of me. It'd be my turn soon.

Sometime around four in the morning if they continued at this speed.

My mind wandered onto Karla and other things. When I came to, somebody else was whining at the table.

We clapped.

During the next two lamentations I devised a plan for financing a new bottle of Cartier perfume. It seemed like a very good one to me. One of the best so far.

I clapped enthusiastically. Those in the front rows turned around.

The performer, a small, haggard-looking man with glasses, who looked as if he might expire at any moment, blushed and bowed slightly in my direction. Now, it was my acquaintance's turn.

When he'd finished his whining, I showed my approval not just by clapping but by stomping my feet on the floor and whistling.

Everybody was looking around.

My acquaintance blushed.

There were three people before the bony poet.

I noticed that all the speakers had dedicated their first poem to the publishers who were such bastards for not wanting to publish their work. From that, there is only one step to self-publishing, like Poet. Maybe he, too, had been a member of such a circle in his youth, how would I know? I looked around. There were no publishers to be seen. Who were they reading this to?

Themselves.

Again, we clapped a bit.

Two more people.

Applause.

One more.

Her.

I concentrated. Looked her in the eyes.

She sat down at the table and started to read from the sheets in front of her. She had a beautiful, slightly husky and very gentle voice.

She didn't dedicate her first poem to the publishers, even though she hadn't been published either, which made me like her even more.

Her poems weren't bad. There was something that made them stand out from the other lamentations. After three millennia of paper scratching it's very hard to write poems about emotions, about the nuances of feeling inside you, without resorting to whining. She finished and I raised my hands to applaud loudly, when a guy sitting in front of me got up. The previous reader. He was wearing a hat, one of those variations on hats worn by soldiers fighting for the Confederacy in the American Civil War, wherever that may be.

I'd applauded him earlier. By mistake. In fact I was applauding my plan for getting another bottle of Cartier perfume, but he appropriated my self-congratulation for himself.

He started speaking.

I couldn't believe it.

Everybody listened to him respectfully, with full attention. Even those who'd already dozed off, waiting for their turn. The head of the circle?

"First, I have to say that this is an example of typically female poetry. Yes, typically female."

He looked around him.

Into my eyes, too. Eyes that could kill.

"And that, of course, is inferior poetry per se. It lacks something which is characteristic of all good male poets. Divine inspiration."

Another look around. Everybody was agreeing.

I felt like a kettle, full of steam. I was boiling, bubbling with fury.

And pure horror joined the anger.

Where am I? Are they serious? Which day is it today? Which year, century?

A sharp chord from an electric guitar cut through my head. A wave from the past.

All the world cannot be wrong
must be me I don't belong . . .

The guy continued.

"Yes, divine inspiration. Women write poetry while in emotional turmoil. When their boyfriend has walked out and so forth. A poet gets up. Early in the morning. He goes into the countryside. Lies on the grass under a tree. He has a pencil and a sheet of paper with him. In pure, unspoiled nature, in the bliss of a new morning, he experiences an inspiration, which I call divine inspiration. And only thus can true poetry be created, the essence of pure beauty."

I was looking at his face, and in my mind it began mingling with the face of an old man, an academic of high culture. Even their voices seemed to be alternating. First one face would talk with the voice of the other and then vice versa. Oh, these young poets.

Hahahaha ha ha!!!

I looked at her. She didn't seem upset. She was calmly watching the speaker.

He shut up.

Everybody applauded.

Him.

She got up and left. She pushed the door open, gently. The speaker took his seat.

I tapped him on the shoulder. He looked back into my sincerely enthusiastic face.

"Congratulations! Congratulations! Well said."

I offered him my hand.

He took it.

"Really wonderful."

I squeezed his hand.

"Divine inspiration! That's what I really liked."

Slowly, with pleasure I started to squeeze my fingers together. Strongly.

"Female poetry! That was good, too."

Even stronger.

"Pure nature, yes."

With all my strength.

"The essence of beauty, that was the best."

I was interested to see whether I'd have enough strength to break a few of his bones. Probably not.

He was getting taller and taller. His body jerked. He was wriggling in his chair. He didn't want to scream with pain. Anything else but scream.

Silently he looked around for help.

Everybody was asleep again. A few insomniacs were listening to the whining at the table.

He groaned. In a muffled, throaty sort of way.

Tears poured from his eyes. Ran down his cheeks and gathered into half-moon shaped puddles at the bottom of his glasses.

The man at the table finished reading his last poem.

We clapped. Everyone, that is, apart from the head of the circle. He pressed his hands onto his balls and bent forward, maybe expecting to be hit as well. I let him nurse his wounded limb at the source of divine inspiration and stepped outside. I closed the door firmly behind me. If I'd had a hammer and some nails, I'd have permanently nailed the door shut.

The poet was still there. She was slowly finishing her cigarette, looking out onto the lit-up street through the window.

I approached her. Leaned on the left edge of the window. Lit a cigarette and gazed through the windowpane.

Squashing that guy's hand wasn't the right thing to do. I know that you have to fight words with words, often without success. Force proves nothing. My only excuse was that the man had every chance of becoming a bigwig. In a few years he'd have worked his way up. He'd be protected by his status. He couldn't be defeated by words or hands. There's permanent peace up there. So it was necessary to beat him now, while he was still young.

I spoke, still turned towards the window.

"Maybe he's sorry now. When I was leaving he had tears in his eyes."

I got a cramp in my right hand, so I began stretching and massaging it.

She turned towards me. Looked at my face, then at my hand and my face again, and said, "Really?"

I turned towards her. Caught a smile in her eyes.

"Really," I confirmed and put on the most innocent smile I could muster.

"Is this your first time in this library?"

"Yes, the first and last time. A friend talked me into coming here."

"Me, too."

She put her cigarette out on the windowsill. Leaned back on the wall and turned the light off with her shoulder. She didn't turn it back on.

A police car drove past with its siren on. The blue light flashed at us nervously. The siren moved off. We were silent, watching each other in the intervals of light and darkness caused by car headlights.

"You are upset nevertheless." I broke the silence. It didn't sound like blasphemy. It wasn't that kind of silence.

"Well you know, these things are very personal. When you write you expose yourself."

"If you have anything to expose," I added. "And you have."

We fell silent again.

Another police car.

"Let's forget this shit," I said. "Let's kiss a little."

It seemed to me that I could see surprise in her eyes in the next beam of light. She said neither yes nor no. She didn't move away when I came closer.

I kissed her lightly on her slightly parted lips. Ran my hand through her hair. I liked her scent. I slid my fingers across her skin, and the response of her skin, the sensation under my fingertips gave me pleasure, too. I kissed her again. She opened her mouth. We teased each other with our tongues. With my left hand, I uncovered her shoulder and the light shone on it. I slid my fingers into the opening of her dress, caressed her breasts, slight bulges around pointy nipples. She was good at the tongue game. We got on very well. I pressed her against the wall, which was covered with books from floor to ceiling. And there, in one and the same place, were the two things I like most.

Books and women.

Not necessarily in that order.

While still kissing her I pulled up her thin skirt. My palms traveled right up the inside of her legs until I touched the hairs peeping out of her panties. I was considerably taller than she was, which necessitated some special maneuvers on my part. I moved my palms back down and again slid them up her thighs. Faster and faster I circled towards the hairs but touched them only in passing, always quickly moving away again. My prick threatened to burst through my zipper. My trousers rose into a bulge between my legs. We pressed against each other. She wasn't passive anymore, she put her arms around me and bit into my neck.

She moved her head away and said, "No, please."

While her body said yes.

I grabbed her behind. It was small and firm. I lifted the poet up. We looked at each other. I asked, "Why not?" And let her slide down my body. With her pelvis over the bump on my trousers.

She sighed deeply. I repeated the maneuver. Looked in her eyes. They were cloudy.

"No," she whispered. More with a shake of her head than her voice.

I let her down the slide.

Lifted her up again.

"Why, don't you like it?"

Down again.

"Please," she whispered so pleadingly that I stopped. Her body was definitely willing. I put my arms around her shoulders and we sat on the windowsill. She pressed herself against me.

"I'd feel like a whore tomorrow morning, you know. At home there's a man I love, with our child, waiting for me. It does feel good, but I'd have such a moral hangover tomorrow."

"I understand." I offered her a cigarette. She accepted it and we lit up.

"But look, I see it all as a game. I like being here with you, kissing, fondling you. We don't have to fuck, just be together. So . . ."

"Yes, I know, but I can't look at it like that. Maybe I take it all too seriously. Maybe all women are like that, I don't know."

We slowly finished our cigarettes. A wave of applause came from inside the room.

"I've earned it."

She smiled and agreed.

"Really, thank you."

She put out her cigarette. She smoked faster than me.

She paused a few inches from my face.

"I'm going," she said softly and apologetically. If I'd reached for her and pulled her towards me, she'd have stayed.

Our lips touched.

Very, very gently.

She stepped towards the door. Paused in the streetlight. We looked at each other. Again I caught a smile in her eyes. She said, "You really do kiss well."

"Yes, I regularly attend the literary evenings."

"And you read Raymond Chandler," she added over her shoulder and disappeared.

Another round of applause.

I liked her. Only now for real. I turned towards the window. With a single drag I finished the rest of my cigarette. Burned a bit of the filter. I couldn't see her. She didn't go down the street. She must live in the other direction.

And again a bittersweet sadness. A quiet regret. When we meet next time, if there is a next time, it won't be the same. It'd never be the same again. I'd tried it before. I put the cigarette out on the window and left.

Fuck it, nothing but leaving all the time. I'd like to know how we ever find the time to arrive so often.

The night was all car headlights and colliding with passersby. I went towards the campus. Juggling with numbers of blocks of flats, floors, and rooms in my head, trying to visualize the faces of the girls I knew behind these combinations of numbers. I soon gave up. When I got there I'd rely on my sight and compare the pictures with the ones I remembered. I didn't feel like going into any bars. I did, however, look through the windows into the well-lit rooms. Maybe I'd see another beer. A crowd of people had gathered in front of the cinema for the last performance. A little bit away from the crowd stood Selim, leaning on the wall. He had his left side turned towards me. His right hand was hidden behind his body.

He greeted me.

I gingerly returned the greeting and added, "Did you cut it badly?"

The hand came out of its hiding place. The bandage shone in the light from an advertisement panel.

He blushed like a tomato.

I started to give him fatherly advice.

"Hey, you don't steal posters just like that. Smashing the glass with your bare hands. Couldn't you have picked up a stone at least?"

His embarrassment was subsiding, the blood was draining from his head.

"I don't know what came over me. I went past the cinema on the way to my room at the dormitory, and I saw it there. I went nearer and looked at her. And then suddenly I was holding her in my hands. Only the broken glass under my feet woke me up. In my room I noticed the blood on my hand and then drops of blood in the corridor."

I asked a woman who was lighting up with her back towards us for a cigarette, and she gave me one.

"Are you coming to the cinema with me?" he asked.

I looked in the direction of the campus, then back at Selim. I nodded. He went to buy a ticket for me. He'd been clutching his in his left hand all along.

I finished my cigarette. A stream of people started moving towards the entrance. I joined in and met Selim half way. I stepped through the entrance sheltered by his wide shoulders. I noticed a look which the woman collecting tickets gave to her colleague opposite.

They both found it hard to stop themselves from laughing.

We sat down and made ourselves comfortable.

I looked at Selim's profile and wanted to color it red.

"Well, Selim, fourth time lucky, eh?"

I succeeded. A wonderful color. He was saved from my gloating look by the darkness, interrupted only by the ray of light running from the film projector towards the screen.

He'd been to all three previous performances of this film. It was only when the opening sequence started rolling that I realized which movie I was watching. The title was *Maria's Lovers*. It starred Nastassja Kinski. The same one as in *Tess*. During the performance, I kept looking sideways at Selim's profile, which looked completely still as if it was carved out of stone. He was somewhere else, wherever that may be. When the lights came on he got up like a sleepwalker and went out. I followed him past the illuminated poster. I was half-expecting him to smash the glass. It didn't happen.

We walked side by side to the bus station. I felt that any moment now he would say something, so I stayed. My presence didn't seem to disturb him.

From time to time I caught him opening his mouth and moving his tongue.

Nothing but unrecognizable semivowels came out. And even those only occasionally and very quietly.

We got on the bus. Sat down. Selim paid for my ticket as well as his. The radio was playing old Italian *canzones*, which were dusting the air with sugar.

Halfway through one of the songs, the conductor announced a ten-minute break. The driver switched off the engine and got off with the conductor for a smoke. Three passengers followed them, ten were either asleep or too drunk, or simply didn't have the will to move. Selim still wasn't saying anything.

I remembered a walk home. From school, when I was quite a few years younger, in the dusk, with a school friend. We both had images of our first loves constantly twinkling before our eyes, the girls for which you had to fall heroically. Silence, when each of us really wanted to talk about our own girl, but hesitated for fear of being teased by the other one. But you talk, sooner or later, all longing. You just can't keep the words to yourself. Selim was staring in front of him as if the screen was still there.

Somebody threw up. A sour stench spread through the bus.

I looked at the driver and the conductor. They hadn't heard anything. They were talking lazily, shuffling and swaying in the cold spring night. The old man didn't show any sign of life.

"Selim, give me your jacket." I tugged at his tatty denim jacket. He looked at me with surprise. Not so much because of my demand but because of the realization that I was there, next to him. I repeated my request with an impatient, demanding voice.

He did what I asked.

I ran out. The driver looked at me with surprise. The conductor was pissing in the corner of a closed bar. I rushed down the street. The church bell struck midnight. I didn't have a plan. One of those moments when I felt like an observer. From somewhere else, I was watching my body doing its own thing. Down the avenue of trees to a cinema. On the wall, a row of illuminated display cases proclaimed COMING SOON. I wrapped the jacket around my right hand, jumping along the row of posters. I came to the right one and smashed it. The sound of glass breaking followed me as I ran up the avenue with my trophy in my hands. The bus was waiting with its engine on. I jumped aboard. The door closed behind me.

I felt like a bank robber.

Selim was looking at me with surprise over the back of his seat. Out of breath, I sat next to him and shoved the poster onto his lap. He straightened it and looked at Nastassja fastening her stocking with her leg raised. He was over the moon. In heaven. I could already feel beer sliding down my throat.

I unwrapped the jacket from my hand. Fragments of glass fell to the floor.

I removed the bigger fragments embedded in the material and threw the jacket onto his lap.

"Thank you," he said. An outburst of gratitude.

"Any time," I nodded manfully. Leaned back as if it had nothing to do with me. I went to sleep for half an hour and left Selim on his own.

We stood at the bus station, looking at the foundry buildings snaking in front of us. The bus disappeared into the night.

He invited me in with him.

The dormitory was in darkness. The warden was dozing

by the turned-down radio in his hut. He had no fingers on his right hand and one leg missing.

I waited outside.

Selim greeted him politely. The warden muttered something unfriendly and looked at Selim's jacket to see if any of the pockets held anything in the shape of a bottle.

Selim deliberately walked up the stairs noisily. He unlocked his door and closed it. Then he tiptoed back down and opened a window in the corridor.

He pulled me up. We crept to his room. Something stank. He switched on the light. There was a made-up bunk next to the wall on the right, obviously his. In the other bunk, under the window, Selim's roommate slept, fully dressed but with no shoes.

"I'm finding it hard to get used to him," he complained, looking at the socks sticking out from under the cover. The source of the stench. "I've been alone in the room for a year and a half."

I took a good look at the sleeping man. The light didn't bother him, at least he didn't move. He was thin and bony, quite a bit younger than Selim and me. Wearing what was probably his grandfather's suit, or at least his father's. New fodder for the foundry. I looked at Selim, who was still shaking his head, and immediately forgot the novice's face. I took another good look at the sleeping man's face, looked away, and again forgot it immediately. I repeated the whole procedure a few more times; the game was quite entertaining. His face was so forgettable.

"When did he arrive?" I asked.

"I don't know, he wasn't here in the morning."

We sat down on the bed.

"Wait," he said and crept out into the corridor. I heard him knocking next door. A sleepy, angry voice could be heard together with his. He came back with a bottle of schnapps.

I was already holding one in my hands.

He looked at me with surprise.

"The novice had it in his bag." I pointed to the blue satchel, lying next to the bunk.

We took a sip first from one then the other bottle. The one that Selim had brought was immediately put aside. It contained some mass-produced malodorous brew of the worst quality.

"Ibro's bottle is full of homemade stuff," I explained.

I had to tell him how I knew the newcomer's name. I got up and turned the bag so that the front was showing. In the middle, under the zipper, there was a nametag written in pencil: "Ibro Hadžipuzić, Dolnje Vrbopolje."

"No house number," said Selim, as if that explained everything.

I sat back down.

"At least he'll be able to tell you what Mecca's like."

"A Muslim," said Selim quietly, shaking his head. "He'd have been better staying where he came from than coming to croak in this foundry."

The schnapps was superb. Smooth and gentle while running down your throat, but a real explosion of heat in the stomach. I switched off the light. The floodlights at the foundry gave off enough light. Slowly, we sipped the schnapps. The uninterrupted rattling of the trolleys loaded with iron ore covered our silence.

The night became red. They'd opened a furnace.

Selim got up, searched for a key in his pocket, and unlocked a wardrobe by the bed. There were three pairs of jeans and a denim jacket hanging inside. And nicely folded T-shirts and underwear. He looked for another, slightly smaller key on a ring, bent over, and unlocked a drawer at the bottom of the wardrobe. The room was still completely lit up. In the drawer there was a bundle of letters in a clear plastic bag. At the bottom there was a poster, folded so that Nastassja's face was at the top, and on top of that a pistol. A German Walther from the Second World War. He reached for the poster for *Maria's Lovers*. He folded it, lifted the pistol, put the poster at the bottom of the drawer, and covered it again with the black metal.

He locked the drawer and closed the wardrobe.

Sat back down. Took a sip from the bottle.

"My father took that gun from an SS officer. He didn't have anything else to give me when I left for here."

The bottle was in my hands again. The night was fading.

I got up and opened the window. He nodded encouragingly. The room was filled with fresh air and the noise of the machinery.

A crane was moving under the foundry roof.

"I knew somebody else would come. Mehmed went home the day before yesterday. Thirty years he'd been here." He was speaking slowly, as if he was reading a bedtime story to a child. "I looked at him when he was leaving and I said to myself, You'll be like that. Dried out from the fire, bent over, and unwell. And then some Ibro will come to replace you. Fuck, is that all that's left?"

This rhetorical question was pronounced louder. Ibro turned in his bed and murmured something.

It didn't sound like an answer.

"And then I went to the cinema," added Selim, and the story was finished.

We emptied the rest of the bottle without talking. The schnapps went to my head. I leaned out the open window and spat. There was a small radio on the table. I switched it on. I started singing in time with a woman's voice from the little box. Quietly first, then louder and louder. Selim was staring at something in front of him and didn't care.

I was bellowing.

"Ah those sleepless nights, they break my heart in two yodel-e-hu-hu yodel-e-hu-hu . . ."

It was beautiful. Ibro shot up. He crouched on all fours in the middle of the bed looking like a sheep. He didn't have a clue what was going on.

He'd get used to it.

Something came flying at the wall. Somebody shouted in the next room, "Shut up motherfucker. I've got work in the morning."

He was right. There's always work in the morning.

Selim was sitting motionless, cradling the empty bottle in his lap. I stepped outside. Closed the door behind me. Ibro was still foulmouthing.

Frankie was singing *Strangers in the Night* on the radio. If I had a voice like Frankie I'd do nothing but sing all my life. I wouldn't think at all.

Just sing.

The corridor window I'd got in through was open.

I jumped out as if I had a horse parked below. It didn't hurt too much.

I rolled in the dust, shook it off my clothes, and pressed my hands on the wall.

I looked at my palms.

They were red.

CHAPTER 3

Sunday morning is made for a bit of music. And for food. I rummaged under the bed for the cassette player and put it on the table. Searching for the only cassette took much longer. I found it in the bathroom, behind the toilet. For the life of me I couldn't remember when I'd put it there.

The on button was a bit stiff and resisted the pressure of my finger. I turned it on with a well aimed karate chop with the edge of my palm.

There were times when I'd always carry that cassette with me, in my top pocket, and record a piece that I liked at the time, while visiting a girl or an acquaintance. I'd record over the things I didn't like anymore. Because of the different lengths of songs, the whole tape consisted of short fragments, usually beginnings and ends of different pieces of music. If I got really tired of it, I'd sell it as a special edition in celebration of the thirtieth anniversary of rock'n'roll.

I took a shower. I shook and squeezed the Cartier bottle. Nothing at all came out. I put on my underpants and moved the door on the wardrobe.

It'd had broken hinges even when I first got it. Inside,

there were two nails, and on them, two hangers. I hung the combat jacket and my trousers on the empty hanger and took my Sunday suit off the other hanger and put it on.

The suit consisted of blue overalls with a jacket: the foundry-workers' uniform, with an emblem consisting of a gold hammer sewn onto the breast pocket.

The road was empty. Folk Muzak of different nationalities and the smell of wiener schnitzel, chips, and mixed salad floated through open windows. A spring Sunday. When you'd like to be somewhere else. Anywhere but here. And when you're there you want to be somewhere else again.

Anywhere but there. And so on.

I looked around for the guard and climbed over the fence.

I avoided factory halls, jumping over tracks, trying to avoid trolleys with red hot ingot moulds. Workers poured out of one of the buildings. I joined them. Became one with the crowd. Here I am, all yours. Oh, motherland!

For the next hour.

They were all women. Mainly older, ugly, and fat. Rough and revolting. From behind, you couldn't distinguish them from men. Women without womanhood.

We formed a line along the wall of the canteen, each holding a tray in our hands. Quite a bit further along, almost at the counter where the food was handed out, I noticed a girl's face. It stood out from the others in the line so strongly it hurt me. I felt real physical pain in my eyes. I'd never seen her before. She must've been a newcomer. She took her tray to a table and sat down. There was an empty chair next to her. I started to push the mighty back in front of me impatiently, but nothing could speed things up. When I got my portion of the bean broth, the chair was already taken. I took a thick wad of luncheon vouchers from my pocket and paid for the food with one of them. Happy that at least for these I wouldn't have to go into action for a while. I sacrificed another voucher for a bottle of beer.

I sat at the row of tables next to hers. Broke a slice of bread. We looked at each other. For longer than an ordinary look of two faces passing in a crowd. I was wondering whether to smile or not. I moved the muscles around my mouth. Too late. She was already down at the steaming bowl. A group of her noisy colleagues surrounded me and separated us. I couldn't see her anymore.

Had I had a newspaper with me I'd have read it. I was eating the sort of food that didn't need any attention. Whoring sort of food. You satisfy a physical need, then you go. There's no foreplay with a bite, no loving lick of the spoon, no gentleness or pleasure.

I stared at the menu for the next day. Today a bean broth with sausage, tomorrow pork ribs in sauce. Which meant they'd put some ribs in this broth and stew it again. On Tuesday Hungarian ribs. They'd add some hot paprika to the leftovers of the broth from Monday, boil it, and dish it out.

That's the way the story goes.

I left the sausage in the bowl. I still wasn't so desperate that I would eat fragments of fat, gristle, bones and other garbage wrapped in a condom.

I stretched my neck and looked between the two people sitting opposite. The girl was still eating.

I stayed seated and amused myself by looking at the woman in front of me. She was of an indeterminate age, one of those women who are never really old or young, whose only wish in childhood, it seems, is to grow up to look like their mother as soon as possible. She was toothless and terribly hungry. She was attacking a sausage, trying to tear off a piece. The rest of the sausage was sticking out of her mouth, dangling about.

Obviously she didn't know how to use a knife and fork. All this intense, wanton battling resembled a parody of sex. It was both funny and revolting.

I got up, took the tray to the hatch, and pushed it through. On my way to the exit, the girl and I looked at each other once more. Eyes, oh what eyes she had. You could drown in them. Large and boundless. I was falling into them. I knocked a woman's broth out of her hands just as she was sitting down. I caught the bowl with my thumbs pushed almost to the bottom of the broth. It splashed on her trousers. I wasn't in the mood for persuasion or argument.

I gave her one of my vouchers and apologized. She didn't grumble too much at all. She put away the voucher and started eating the remnants in the dish. I wiped my fingers on my trousers. A look back. The girl was looking at me but immediately looked away. I was angry with myself for having been so clumsy. The reflex of a hunk on a beach who struts with his lungs full of air in front of the admiring girls and then trips over something hidden in the sand and falls.

I stopped outside the door and leaned on the fence.

I bummed a cigarette. When the woman offered me a match, too, I refused, saying, "I've got my own, thank you."

She came out. The only one around who looked like a woman in spite of the sexless blue dress that fell to her knees. Below that, beautiful legs in black tights. She leaned on the fence at the other side of the stairs, slightly lower down. We smiled at each other. I went to her and asked her for a light. With a lighter she lit my cigarette first, then hers. I was falling into her eyes. She said, "Any time."

The moment between her opening her mouth and her voice coming out seemed like eternity. A terrible fear. There are women who, however attracted you may be to them because of their looks, spoil everything when they open their mouths. Some get over that hurdle okay. The ruin comes later, with the meaning of their words. Maybe that's what I was frightened of, I don't know.

I nodded and returned to the other side. Very rarely had a woman disturbed me so much. First, because of the surroundings. Looks are what you see first. But there was something else, something radiant. Spiritualists would call it a spirit. That's what I couldn't understand. Considering where she worked, she shouldn't have had one.

But I wasn't convinced. She confused me. I would've died if I'd found out that her eyes were so deep only because there was nothing behind them. I realized I was staring at her. I looked away, greeted acquaintances. My eyes kept going back in the intervals. Her eyes, too. She looked at her watch, put out the cigarette, and set off back to work. I followed her, a meter behind. She didn't look back. We were in the same group of women with which I'd come to the canteen. They sat down at the conveyor belt, which was going faster and faster. She was sitting at the end of the line. Small packets full of nails were sliding past her, already sealed. She pressed a large stamp with the date and a code on them. Her colleague, sitting a meter ahead of her, counted the packets.

One two three four five six seven eight nine ten.

Counted again.

Changed the boxes.

She was mouthing the numbers without a sound, as with a rosary.

Thud thud thud thud thud thud thud thud thud thud fell the packets from a pipe.

Stamp stamp stamp stamp stamp stamp stamp stamp stamp stamp went the girl who I couldn't take my eyes off.

One two three four five six seven eight nine ten, counted her colleague. A new box.

Every stamp filled me with a new horror. Fucking hell, these two are here only because they are cheaper than a machine. Cheaper than an automated stamper and a photocell that would count. This was true about all the women in the hall. A sea of bodies.

She turned around and looked at me.

Her eyes.

My God, I'm falling in love with a machine.

Stamp stamp stamp stamp stamp stamp stamp stamp stamp stamp went her hand.

For ever and ever. Amen.

I wanted to shout, "Hey, watch out, the machine will get you!"

But I didn't say anything. I went out. Quickly, nearly ran out.

The noise of the falling nails stayed behind.

I leaned my head on the wall and wanted to throw up.

I changed my mind and suppressed my disgust. A shame to waste two vouchers.

I went to my flat so depressed I could only lie down and stare at the ceiling. But before that I undressed. I held the overalls between two fingers and hung them back in the wardrobe. Moved the door back into its place.

Firmly.

I wasn't horrified by the fact that most people were like machines. There was something else about all the people I knew, men and women, who worked at the foundry or anywhere else, that made me shudder.

A quiet, calm satisfaction.

With everything.

It's not such a problem to stamp and stamp and get a salary at the end of each month. It's not really work.

All of a sudden I loved them all. Those others. Hippy, Poet, Noodle somewhere there in the hills, all of them.

I fell asleep.

When I woke up, not long after I went to sleep, I thought I'd had a nightmare.

There was a smell of lunch coming from all the flats.

Just the right time for going to the National Library.

I walked a long distance along the fence to the opening for the railway tracks. I jumped from sleeper to sleeper, cut through the foundry, then across the bridge over a river far below, and came to the other side. At the foot of a mountain ridge that, like its neighbor opposite, had forced the foundry to grow only lengthwise. I went past the old, abandoned workshops and warehouses, rusting trucks.

I stopped in front of the National Library.

A huge mountain of used paper which the foundry bought by the ton. The long wooden shed intended for storing the paper was too full. The side wall had collapsed under the pressure. The paper spilled out. A chain of paper mountains rose above the bodies of rusted car parts piled into heaps. Our nation's mourned literary and automotive treasures.

Smoke was coming from the side of the hill. There was a Gypsy settlement on the hill, and this mountain of paper and steel was their shopping center. Every Sunday I'd see them — usually children — rummaging through the cars, scrap metal, and paper. They'd pile their catch on a trolley and take it home. The next day they would sell back to the foundry everything except any of the more useful or slightly more valuable parts, which they sold to mechanics or anybody else who might be interested in them. The fence was rusty and full of holes. I looked around the yard, even though there was no need to be afraid of the guard. There was only one man guarding all the scrap yards. An old man. Once, he must have been a giant. One of his legs had been cut off in the middle of his thigh. All his strength was now trapped by the clumsiness of his wooden-legged walk.

I went in bent over, a suitable entry into such a distinguished establishment. Walking on paper mountains demands special skills. You're constantly losing the ground from under your feet. You can slide back by meters, there's nothing to hold on to. You have to go on all fours. That's how it is with paper.

I got to the shed by crawling on top of the mountains. Outside, there were newspaper and cardboard, inside this and that, as they call books around here.

At the shed door stood a large paper press for compressing the paper into enormous rolls, out of which you can't get anything, because it's all packed so tight.

I started rummaging, searching without aim. You can get real pleasure out of that. Every discovery is a pleasant surprise. I had a list of comics in my head I could sell to the brats in the blocks of flats. Some of them were passionate collectors.

My eyes got used to the semi-darkness. I discovered two Gypsy girls who'd hidden in the corner of the shed, frightened of the guard. We'd met before. They carried on calmly. They were collecting the heaviest paper and tying it into bundles. They'd carry them over to their trolley and bring them back again the next day.

They resembled each other. Probably sisters. The older one was tall and the younger smaller and slightly chubby. Indeterminate ages.

Children in the bodies of grown up women. I met quite a few here on Sundays. None of them lasted long. Their stomachs would start growing, and they'd stop coming.

I was knee deep in the well-known novels of social realism. This style must have once been very popular around here. I opened a thick, threadbare book. Read the first sentence:

"In Moscow lives a leader, who is fairer and wiser than any other born on this Earth, our comrade Stalin . . ."

I looked at the author's name on the cover. I'd never heard of him.

I threw the book away and rummaged on. I pulled out a first edition of Meyrink's *The Golem* from 1913. It went in my pocket.

The Gypsies were picking through the pile non-stop. They didn't seem to see me as competition. After an hour's rummage, I only had a couple hundred grams of paper on me.

The younger Gypsy brought another bundle of, judging by the effort she was putting into it, heavy magazines to her sister. She threw it on the heap.

Her sister got a piece of string ready. From the top a face familiar from somewhere was looking at me.

I pretended to approach them accidentally and made sure. It was a *Playboy*. Nastassja Kinski was on the front cover.

Suddenly, I became thirsty. I thought of beer. Or of Selim, I should say.

And I foolishly said without thinking, "Hey, how much do you want for that magazine?"

What a mistake! I became aware of it even before I finished my question. They looked at me with surprise. It must have been something very important to have made me talk to them for the first time since we started meeting here. They looked at the magazine and then at me again.

"How much are you offering?" the younger one asked.

So it'd be her and me negotiating. The older one didn't interfere, she just looked on with amusement.

"I'll help you carry the paper home."

She laughed at me cheekily. I put on an I-couldn't-care-less expression and a slight smile. I spoke with a deep voice, hiding impatience, which I couldn't get rid of. I was hoping at least it didn't show. I could let them take the mag home and then re-sell it again the next day. There was a ninety-nine percent chance that that was what would happen. But it was that one percent that fucked me up. I didn't want to risk it. It was I who had gotten myself into this bargaining, and it would be I who had to carry on to the end. The find would be worth a case of beer to Selim.

She picked up the magazine and waved Nastassja in front of my eyes. A red flag to a bull.

"I want money. How much?"

"I haven't got money."

"Forget it then."

She threw the magazine back. The sister started pulling the string.

"Okay."

My surrender.

"How much?" she asked.

I told her the amount. Two beers from Selim's crate. Immediately, I became aware of my second mistake. I just couldn't get it right. I should've done it differently. She should've said the price. I would've moaned a bit, trying to lower it. We would've reached an agreement. But I was the first to say the price and now it was her who was bargaining. In the other direction. Up.

She said half a crate.

I shook my head to say that was too much and started rummaging through the paper again, moving towards the exit.

I'd let them know the mag was worth something. They knew me that much. They knew that there was very little I took with me. This wasn't about its weight.

"All right," I heard from behind me.

I went back to them.

"Give me the money," she said, looking at me hungrily and holding the magazine next to her hip so that I couldn't grab it from her and run.

I admitted, "I haven't got it on me."

Added, "I can bring it back in an hour."

It would work. Selim wasn't at work. A quick run to the dormitory and back.

"If you haven't got the money now, you can buy it next week. We'll bring it with us."

I didn't quite get the purpose of that move. She probably wanted to gain time and ask around to find out the true value of the magazine. Most probably I would get it in seven days because they could never sell scrap paper at that price. Everybody'd laugh at them. It wasn't hardcore porn, which you could sell for quite a bit at the dormitories. On top of it all, I was really getting into this trading business now. The matter was becoming more personal by the minute. My success or failure.

"I'm not interested. I want it today or never."

They weren't too sure why the hurry.

She found the only probable explanation.

"Oooooooh," — I hated these prolonged *oooooooohs* — "you're desperate? You'd like to jerk yourself off?"

She opened the magazine.

"Go ahead, I'll turn the pages for you."

Selim, if this succeeds, I'll want two crates.

I didn't react. I watched her with a smile. A cool guy. She'll finish her performance. There was no point in interrupting her. It could make her angry.

"What's the matter? Haven't you got it in your hands yet? Don't you like the pictures? Look here, some different ones."

She turned a page.

"Still nothing? Would you like to be on your own?"

Her sister was very amused, or so it seemed.

Act two.

"Sir is not satisfied with ordinary mortals. He wants actresses." She closed the magazine, turned the front cover with Nastassja towards me, and put it in front of her face. With her left hand she held the magazine, while she lifted her flowery skirt with her right hand and showed me her cunt.

"Do you like it better this way?"

She started moving her hips. Her tits were shaking beneath her dirty yellow T-shirt.

She was sighing, "Oh ooh oh ooooh . . ."

Her sister was dying with laughter, without a single sound coming out of her mouth.

It didn't look that bad at all. Not erotic, more funny. Nastassja's face on the imbalanced and short, rather tubby body. With a hand grabbing between her legs and scratching her pubic hair.

The guard entered the shed.

The performance ended.

We looked down at him from the top of the heap of paper. When we saw that he was making his way up the paper hill, we started running away towards the fallen wall. We weren't hurrying too much. We were only trying to run because of the feeling that it's right to run when you're trying to escape.

I was a good meter behind the Gypsies, looking for the opportunity to grab the magazine. That was the only thing she'd taken, holding it with both hands. Her sister was carrying a bundle of paper.

We ran out, balancing on the paper ridge. The younger sister slipped. She tried to regain her balance. She waved her arms in the air. The magazine was in her right hand. I jumped and tried to pull it out of her hand. I missed. I pushed her down the slope. She didn't let go of the magazine. She slid down the paper slide, causing an avalanche which poured behind her.

In the middle of the slope, the chassis of a car was sticking out of the paper.

She was carried towards it.

Her sister had already thrown the bundle over the fence, slid on the paper heap which was as high as the top of the fence, and jumped over to the other side.

Using all my strength, I tried to stay at the top. The avalanche was moving too fast. My feet were giving way beneath me. Everything was moving and slipping down.

It carried me after the girl. She grabbed hold of the edge of the chassis and tried to get away from the main stream of the avalanche. She didn't let go of the magazine. Damn stubbornness.

Scrambling with both feet, she managed to move away from the avalanche.

The pressure of the paper had slightly shifted the chassis.

I slid past on my back. My feet touched the ground. Immediately I jumped forward to avoid the paper slide that was just about to bury me.

I landed on my stomach. Everything was calm now. The silence was shocking.

I rolled over and looked up.

The other sister was out. She stood there looking at the

center of the slope. The moving chassis, having no firm support for its weight, pressed on the girl, who was half buried in paper. Her hands started to scatter the paper sheets. She tried to dig herself out. She didn't quite succeed.

Her right ankle remained under the edge of the chassis. She'd tucked the *Playboy*, which she'd been clutching in her hand all along, under her T-shirt. She tried to rescue her foot. She pulled the paper from under it.

It didn't help. The metal kept sinking in. She tried to lift it. There was no support for her anywhere. She stopped moving and looked at her sister.

Asking for help with her eyes.

Her sister didn't see her.

Her eyes were glued to the limping guard, who appeared at the top of the ridge by the fallen wall of the shed.

He stopped.

Everything was frozen. Everybody was waiting for the first move.

At last he caught on. Something he'd been waiting for all his life has finally happened. They'd put him there to catch thieves. A very fruitless task if you've only one leg. Children used to come to tease him. They'd let him almost catch them and then run away. They toyed with him.

He wasn't swearing like he usually did. He roared like a dragon. Launched forward forgetting two things.

That he didn't have one leg and that he was walking on paper. He fell and slid by the edge of the shed to the yard full of scrap metal. He got up.

Picked up a piece of metal pipe.

He growled.

I jumped up and climbed towards the girl. The nose of the chassis quivered. She moaned.

I let the paper return me to where I'd begun.

I started climbing in a long parabola that would bring me just above her.

The guard forced his way in a straight line. Over a line of old cars separating him from his aim. It's hard to do acrobatics with a wooden leg.

He realized that wasn't the way to do it.

He scrambled up to the top. He from the left, me from the right. I arrived quite a bit before him. He slipped back a good few times. He wouldn't let go of the metal pipe.

Slowly, with my arms spread wide, I slid down to the girl.

She looked at me with hatred.

"Give," I said.

Reached with my hand.

She spat at it. And then again at my face. The distance between us allowed only a spray to dampen my skin. I wiped my hand on the paper and my face on my sleeve.

Half sitting, half lying, I looked at her calmly.

The guard had finally managed to get to the top. He was crawling on the ridge. His face was a terrifying red mask. The veins on his forehead stood out in knots. He was wheezing. He was slowly approaching the right spot for the descent towards the girl, using the pipe for support.

I looked at the sister. She didn't move.

The girl heard the wheezing and the dull thuds of the pipe against the paper. She twisted her neck in vain. She didn't want to ask me what was happening.

I sat there waiting.

The guard wheezed into her visual field. With my arms spread out and the calm smile of a talk-show host, I introduced the guest on today's show.

She saw him.

He was crawling nearer. He didn't want to descend too early and miss his aim.

He was looking only at her.

He wanted to kill.

To taste blood.

The girl tried to take off. Forgot about the trapped leg.

She displaced a few sheets of paper and gave up.

She looked at me. She was in no doubt. The guard was going to beat the shit out of her. There would be nothing left of her. She'd suffer for all those who'd escaped him.

"Give," I said.

I reached out.

She didn't spit. With a terrible hatred — her eyes bulging with terror — she screamed, "No!!!!!!"

I moved my hand away.

"If you give me the magazine I'll save you."

I calmly added the sentence that cleared her eyes. Changed her expression to that of mistrust.

The guard descended and missed.

The avalanche took him past us towards the left. Almost down to the bottom.

She looked me in the eyes. Took the risk. What else could she do?

She took the magazine from its hiding place.

A short moment of hesitation. Reached out with her hand.

I took the magazine and Nastassja went under my T-shirt.

The girl watched me with fear.

The guard started climbing again. In a small arc towards us.

The girl's leg was trapped under the back wheel arch.

I started pulling the paper from under her.

I had the magazine and could have left. Indeed, I did think of that possibility for a moment. But only for a moment.

The foot wasn't hurt. The chassis kept sinking and pressing the foot into the paper.

I tried to rock the chassis.

But I couldn't find any support.

The whole thing was probably supported by a bale of compressed paper. I didn't have enough time to dig my way to it.

I was beginning to panic. I didn't know how near the guard was.

It seemed to me he was right behind me, growling into my ear. I kept looking towards the front part of the chassis.

With all my strength I tried to lift the back part. The girl was frantically pulling paper from under her foot.

I pushed up but was knocked back down onto the paper.

The guard couldn't be heard.

I stopped and looked around. Everything was frozen.

Blood was pumping in my ears.

Where the fuck is he?

A crow cawed in the woods.

First, I saw a hand grab the front of the chassis.

A moment later a body leaped up.

Screaming, he struck with the pipe.

The girl screamed.

He was too short. He was bent over the car.

The blow had dented the metal. I was covered with flakes of paint from the car and fragments of glass that had been left in the window frame.

He tried to climb on top of the car. Roaring, he kept hitting out with his right hand.

Because of his weight the back of the car lifted.

With all my strength I pushed it up.

It threw me on my ass.

The girl crawled away on all fours at an incredible speed.

The rocking of the car caused another avalanche.

The chassis started to slide down, carrying the guard with it.

I ran away so quickly that the sheets of paper flew around me like virgin snow behind a skier.

The guard slid away, growling with despair. He saw us escape. The party was over. We wouldn't be having any more fun.

He hurled the pipe after us. It flew high above our heads, bounced off the fence, and rattled on the scrap metal.

The front of the car hit the ground. Stood on its end. Ejected the guard in an elegant arc.

At last he shut up. He was waving his arms in the air and opening his mouth. His prosthesis detached. Flew away in a different direction. The empty trouser leg waved at us. It looked as if he was going to hit a wrecked van, but he flew over it onto a heap of newspapers. He dug into it. An avalanche immediately covered him.

The sheets of newspaper settled down slowly.

The sisters stood looking at each other.

I felt for the magazine. It was stashed in my trousers. And the book was in my pocket.

I ran along the fence back towards the town, away from the Gypsies.

Maybe they'd change their minds and call for reinforcements. You never know.

The paper on top of the guard moved, and out popped his head. All you could see were the whites of his bulging eyes. He howled like a factory siren. Foam sprayed from his mouth. His hands, which were trying to dig out his body, threw the torn paper high into the air.

A light breeze blew them around.

Selim, this was worth three crates.

I felt cold, which made me realize I was sweaty. I was completely wet. My balls were swimming in sweat, which was running in torrents down my back. I put off my visit to Selim's till later and went to the flat to have a shower.

The bar was still empty. I sat at a table in the corner and gazed through the window. The waitress peeped out of the kitchen. When she saw who it was, she immediately disappeared again.

The crackly radio played the current pop successes.

First, three pensioners came in. They drank their spritzers, explaining how many people they'd kill and who would be shot if they were presidents of this country. They had a terrible argument about methods of execution. The winner was the one who suggested they should all be covered in honey and thrown on an ants' nest. Having calmed down they ordered another round.

I took Nastassja from under my T-shirt, briefly looked at the photos, turned to the interviews. It was a French edition of *Playboy*. I soon gave up and read only the cartoon captions.

She moved a chair and sat next to me.

"What'll you have?"

Some women really do know how to play the right tune.

She went to get two beers. I tried to remember her name. In vain. All I could remember was that she was easy. It may be true, how should I know. I only knew her by sight. Once we had waited together for a bus, and I'd fucked her twice, both times at a party, pissed out of my head.

We poured the beer and started talking. Had she been born forty years ago, she would've been considered a great beauty. Then, her square face surrounded by curly hair would have been used as the epitome of a heroic Red Army soldier, a young Komsomol who had surpassed her norm by 315%. I looked at her, and martial music rattled through my head. Cheering masses shouted slogans under large banners. Tanks rolled down the roadways. Her face looked out from the turrets. People threw flowers. She reminded me of the screaming pathos of the bright future. Of victories. Only victories.

A terrible bitch.

It wasn't her fault. You're born the way you're born. But I could only force myself as far as medium niceness during our conversation.

She said she was waiting for her boyfriend. She was half an hour early. I felt sorry for her. Real women make their men wait.

I put my elbows on the table and rested my head on them. I was looking at her from below, like at an old movie newsreel.

As if she was aware of my associations, she had even accentuated her face with a shapeless gray jacket and a shitty light brown skirt. Probably a present from her grandmother. She didn't smoke. When I mentioned cigarettes, she went and bought a packet. She didn't have a bad figure. A nice, well proportioned ass. Under the straight-cut loose cardigan, you could just about make out large breasts. Not drooping, judging by her cleavage, which was in the right place. As she was bringing my cigarettes, I noticed knee-high white socks. I sighed sadly. Women who dressed as boringly as that were usually themselves boring.

I looked in front of me. I couldn't stand her loving look. A tender look as if it was intended for newborn kittens. What she wanted most was to cradle me in her arms, stroke me behind my ears. I regretted those two times at the party. Alcohol drives all my blood into my prick. Because there is a law which says that the same thing can't be in two places at once, my brain stays without blood. As my lower head is smaller than the one on top, my intellectual capacities become correspondingly smaller. Thinking of one thing only. Maybe she wasn't a whore and agreed to fuck me only because she wanted to tie me to her. I felt like a bastard.

Oh, justice, where are you these days, we never see you around here anymore.

Poet joined us. Immediately he got a beer.

Your friends are my friends, too. The influence of cowboy stories is still very strong on some people.

I finished my second beer and a third one was already on its way. Poet started rambling. He pulled his latest booklet out of his pocket, turned a few pages, and then started reading, "Soil . . ."

A pause.

"And on it a forest . . ."

I was fiddling with the bottle in my hands. At great length I studied the label and the date on it. I remembered the girl from the foundry. I thought of my malfunctioning glands. One hormone too much, another too little. My feelings come in waves, from happiness to hatred. But most often a mess of bittersweet sadness. Poet only needed his book as a prompt. He wasn't reading anymore but reciting.

"And in the forest, trees . . ."

I looked at our hostess. She was listening to him intently. Whining always finds hearts full of pain and frustration. There's no real what-the-hell-do-I-care attitude in poets like there is in healthy people.

Maybe that's why nobody reads them.

"And on trees, branches . . ."

I was bored to death. I kept turning the empty bottle in my hand. The girl really was in a trance. She didn't notice that my beer was gone. A betrayal in your own contingent.

I looked out on the empty street. I listened to the pensioners, who were going on about putting a stick up "their" asses and roasting "them" over a fire.

It would be good to ask Poet what the title of the poem was. "Botany for Beginners"?

"And on branches, leaves . . ."

I moved to another chair and opened my legs. With my knee I touched her thigh. She didn't move away.

I put my hand on the bare skin. Pulled her skirt up and slid my palm towards the warmth between her legs.

She squeezed her legs and grabbed my hand. Not in defense.

"And the leaves are moving in the wind . . ."

My middle finger, the finger made for knocking on the door when visiting, penetrated first. My index finger didn't want to be left behind.

"To and fro. They touch and then move away . . ."

Poet didn't notice anything. The booklet lay closed on the table.

He was staring at the wall between the girl and me.

"Some meet, others don't . . ."

She tried to stay calm. Motionless. She was biting her lips. She wasn't listening to Poet anymore. My usual flaw. I always want to be the center of attention.

"The wind moves them, the wind carries them away . . ."

She was kneading my arm. Her nails dug into the material of my jacket.

"They go yellow and then they rot away . . ."

Her breathing got shallower and faster.

"That's why we people are like leaves . . ."

Poet raised his voice. The finale was coming. We weren't far behind.

"The wind which brings us closer and then moves us apart . . ."

She grabbed the bulge on my trousers. There was no time to unzip them.

That's why for centuries they used buttons. They tear beautifully in such situations.

"And kills us . . ."

I fixed my eyes on Poet's watch and didn't look around. I didn't care if anybody saw us.

"And what is that, the contact between the leaves?" he asked in a loud voice.

We didn't answer. Only our fingers went faster and faster.

"LOVE !!!" howled Poet.

"LOVE !!!"

"LOVE !!!!!!!!!!!!!!!"

And he collapsed breathlessly onto the table. We were waiting for him there.

We looked at each other, our heads together, out of breath like marathon runners.

"Did you like it?" Poet asked the girl.

"Yes," she breathed and blushed.

"Not bad," I added. He didn't hear my positive tone. He probably wasn't expecting it from me.

Everybody's got a circle of people they turn to when they're hungry for praise. I went to the toilet. I wiped my pants with toilet paper and rinsed my prick under the tap. The water heater wasn't working. The cold deflated my prick in front of my very eyes.

I went back. There was a stranger in my chair.

"We're going," he hurriedly explained.

Indeed, he got up. The girl avoided my eyes. His hair was combed very tidily and covered in brilliantine. He, too, was about forty years behind his time. I looked at their faces and I could only see them in black and white, retouched, slightly faded. A wedding picture in a rococo frame hanging above a marital bed. And on the bed, a doll that says MAMA if you lay her down.

They left. From the door, she sent me the kind of hot and passionate look that the man by her side would probably never receive.

Even housewives sometimes take a walk on the wild side.

Poet looked after them sadly. There went his audience.

I sat back in my chair and lit up. I offered Poet a cigarette, too. We smoked in silence.

I wasn't sure that the girl really had taken the whole thing just as a little distraction from everyday life. I wouldn't want to give her any false hopes.

I'm really not a good person. After the two parties, I had decided to apologize to her and promised myself never to do it again. I did do it for the third time and again I was making the same promises. It was clear to me I wouldn't keep them. I just forgot as I went along. Maybe I should have a career in politics.

"What's this?" asked Poet, gesturing at the magazine. I

turned its front cover up. He reached for it and looked at the centerfold with great pleasure.

I put the magazine under my T-shirt.

I was still upset.

The news had just finished on the radio. Country music was playing. They had started with the right song.

At first I only listened but soon I was singing along loudly. My worry turned into laughter at myself.

"IT'S NOT LOVE BUT IT'S NOT BAD."

The waitress looked out of the kitchen and shouted, "Oi, what's the matter with you? Can't you read?"

With her raised right hand, she pointed above her head. She pointed to the right sign without looking at it.

NO SINGING

Next to it there were many other signs. She could easily have pointed to a different one. A lot of practice is needed for such precision.

"It's all right, Wilhelm," I reassured her and shut up. She disappeared. Besides singing, things like breaking glasses, playing cards, playing chess, spitting on the floor, and giving drinks to those who were already drunk were also not allowed, each rule appearing on a separate sign. I suddenly felt very restricted. I felt like doing all those things one after another, even though they were the sort of things I normally very rarely do, apart from the last thing. Without prohibition, there would be no temptation.

The time had come to say a few words to Poet.

"You know, that poem was very good."

He looked at me with surprise. There was a trace of interest in his eyes.

Maybe I'm not completely lost for art.

"I really liked it," I confirmed.

He still wasn't quite sure that I wasn't bullshitting.

Embarrassed, he mumbled, "Thanks."

I leaned forward.

"Can I ask you something?"

He nodded.

"Have you published your hundredth booklet yet?"

He got worried, expecting a sting in the tail. He hesitated, wondering whether to claim ignorance. Admitted in the end, "The one I just read from is the hundred-and-second."

"May I look at it?"

He gave me the book.

I read the first three poems. With my palm I covered the open pages to stop it from closing, and I looked him in the eyes.

"I've got to tell you something. You know, I haven't read your last thirty books at all. I've been putting them in a heap without even opening them."

He nodded understandingly but with a terrible sadness, completely resigned to his fate.

"I'm regretting it now. I hadn't thought you could still develop. But there's a great difference between the last book I read and this one. This one is much better. As if it hadn't been written by the same person. Just first impressions, of course. When you delve deep into the poems you realize that the themes are the same, just treated on a higher level."

It seemed that I'd defrosted him. He leaned forward trustingly and nodded.

"But! Look!"

I started to leaf through the booklet.

"Cyclostyle. Usually. Sometimes photocopies. Covers made of slightly thicker writing paper. You take it in your hands and there's no temptation to open it. And you think to yourself, another schoolboy writing garbage."

He sighed.

"What can I do? Do you have any idea how expensive printing is these days?"

"I know, I know."

I leaned nearer.

"After a hundred books printed on, forgive the expression, toilet paper, it's time for a real book. Don't you think so?"

An even deeper sigh.

"But they don't want to —"

I interrupted him as if I hadn't heard him.

"Bound in leather. With a protective cover in color. Real print on sparkling white paper of the best quality. On nice, heavy stock. On artist's paper."

He started daydreaming. Quickly I bent over nearer to his ear. Using a voice suited to a terrible last secret, I whispered, "Ninety grams per square centimeter."

He looked at me with confusion.

"Well, the weight of the paper, you know."

He nodded quickly.

"Oh yeah. The weight, yeah."

I leaned back.

"It'd be good if you chose the best poems out of the hundred and two booklets and bring them to me. I'll do the rest. The time has come to look back and draw a line after your first hundred. Do you like the title *Selected Works*? Or would you like something else?"

He didn't understand anything anymore. I hurried on with the explanation.

"My contact can send your manuscripts to the printers. The publishers would publish it even though it's not in their annual plan. My contact would call it an external order from someone who is paying for it himself. Clear?"

He was clear that we were talking money now. Quickly he sobered up.

"How much would it cost?"

I told him the approximate amount.

"That's two months' salary."

The air escaped from his lungs. His shoulders sank.

"You did ask me earlier if I knew how expensive printing was these days."

"I know, but —"

I raised my voice. Changed the tone of it to firmness and decisiveness. My face expressed annoyance and disapproval.

"My dear Poet. If you're unwilling to take risks you'll never get anywhere. It's better to have something firm in your hands than a hundred of these sheets crumpled in your pockets. Do something! Take a risk! Move out of the grayness. Think. A book. A real book. You open it and smell it. There's nothing nicer than the smell of fresh print. And what can you smell now? Toner from the photocopiers."

He hesitated. He agreed with me, it was just the money that was still bothering him.

"I know —" I put my hand on my heart "— you don't trust me. I have a bad reputation. This is what we'll do, if you agree of course."

We put our heads together.

"I've got some savings for a rainy day, you know what I mean? I'll pay for everything. I'll lay the money down for you. In the end, you get five hundred copies, a few advertising posters, an organized book signing, and an invoice. Only then do you pay me. You don't give me a penny before then. Who's taking a risk now? You could tell me to fuck off and all my savings would be just a pile of books in my flat."

He bit his lip. Scratched behind his ear.

"It'll be done in two weeks. No waiting. You know how long you have to wait normally? Years."

Quietly I added, "It's your decision."

He took a good minute before he offered me his hand.

"It's a deal."

I shook his hand.

"You won't let me down?" I asked him again.

"No," he said vehemently and ordered two beers. That's never happened to me before. He was serious. So was I.

We poured the beer.

"Why are you doing this?" he asked me. He didn't dare ask me directly what my cut was.

I answered the unasked question first.

"I won't take anything for myself. You'll get an official invoice with a date and a stamp. You'll pay the exact amount on the invoice. Why am I doing this? I don't know if you'll understand. I'm a real cynic who disdains everything. But you know, I used to write, too, years ago. I stopped. You've either got talent or you haven't. Maybe I'd like to realize my lost ambitions through you. If I can't be a famous poet, I'll at least let you be one, you with talent but without any marketing skills. I'll make my name famous through yours."

He looked at me warmly.

A group of artists walked into the bar. Four men with goatees and the sort of hats that painters wear, and with them two not badly preserved forty-year-old women. Aging groupies. I knew them by sight. Poet belonged to their circle, I didn't. They sat at our table, taking no notice of me. I knew one of them was an amateur painter. He had his own circle, which used to be very popular. The number of members had grown to immeasurable heights. They used to walk the meadows carrying easels and all the rest of the equipment and paint haystacks. They invaded the countryside like biblical locusts. You couldn't piss in a bush or throw a stone over a haystack without hitting one of them. They exhibited their work together and gave advice to each other. But now the number of members was considerably smaller. Paints and canvases are expensive. They'd completely saturated the market; there was a haystack hanging on a wall in every household.

They ordered a round.

I was interested to see whether they were such bastards as to exclude me.

They weren't. I got a beer. One of the women looked at me as if I were a parasitic worm. Once, she must have been a beauty. Now she was only poisonous. She was trying to compensate for the breakdown of her body by enriching her spirit. I wasn't sure that the local artists were the right choice.

They started to let off hot air. I leaned back in my chair and fell asleep with my eyes open. That's one of the most basic facets of polite behavior. Those who don't master it look uncultured.

I woke up during one of their recitations.

"He who sings is blind."

"Oh, so you like Stevie Wonder, too?" I joined the conversation.

They fell silent. As if I'd let out a loud fart at a funeral. They didn't even look at me. The poisonous snake poured hatred on me. Selim and Ibro walked through the door. They sat down a few tables away. I got up, politely said goodbye, nodded to Poet, and went to sit with Selim and Ibro.

They watched me with disgust for joining company of that sort.

Selim introduced me to Ibro. Ibro to me. We shook hands. His hand felt shapeless. Not a soft damp sponge and not a contact with a person of character.

Selim ordered a round. I excused myself for a moment and went to piss.

When I sat down again they were drinking in silence. I wasn't in a hurry.

I asked Ibro, "When do you start work?"

"Tomorrow," he said.

I took the magazine from under my T-shirt and put it face down on the table. They fixed their gaze on a cigarette ad.

I emptied my glass and put it on the table. I took the magazine, pushed it to the middle, and turned it over.

Selim's jaw dropped. His hands reached forward by a whole ten centimeters before he stopped them. I opened the magazine. Slowly, with pleasure, I turned the pages. Looked at Selim's face. When I'd gone past Nastassja, I closed the magazine. The ad lay on the table. I moved my hands away. I lit a cigarette. I've always loved theater. Ibro was looking at us. Selim was staring at the photo of a cigarette packet, his wrists over the table edge.

He was ripe for at least four crates.

I smoked half of the cigarette before he lifted his eyes and looked at me.

He asked, "How much?"

I looked at him with surprise and misunderstanding.

"How much what? Nothing. It's yours."

I shrugged my shoulders and opened my hands. I was asking myself how anybody could be such a bastard.

Had I told him a price, Selim and I would have immediately finished the deal. This way I'd done him a favor and I'd be able to drink half-liter bottles from his gratitude for years.

Slowly he reached for the magazine. Leafed through it once more. Ibro was peering over his shoulder. Selim put the magazine under his T-shirt.

Remained seated.

Suddenly he came to and shouted, "Waitress! Another round!"

We got it. Not just one. One after another. Selim was euphoric. He was blabbing nonsense. He did nothing but drink and piss until closing time. Everything was beginning to get lost in a fog.

"TIME TO GO!!!" shouted the waitress.

Leaning on each other, we stood at the foundry fence.

"Where to?" asked Selim.

"Let's go to the dormitory," suggested Ibro. "I've got dice, we'll play dice."

He pulled some poker dice out of his pocket and showed them to us. We agreed to play. We went to the shop to buy a case of beer and stuffed the bottles in grocery bags. We each carried a bag.

We slowly went to the dormitory. Walking wasn't very easy

for any of us. A local bus came by and stopped at a stop two hundred meters ahead.

"Let's take the bus," Selim shouted and ran.

We followed. I was clumsy with the full bag. It kept hitting me on the knees. Selim was the first at the bus, which was already moving. He said something to the driver, who wasn't listening. He pressed the button to close the doors. Selim grabbed the two closing halves and stopped them. I could see his muscles flexing under his T-shirt. He opened the door. Something in the mechanism made a noise. The driver started shouting. Selim whispered something back. The driver shut up and shrank in his seat. He didn't try to drive off. I reached the bus. I looked back and saw Ibro struggling about twenty meters behind me. A stream of water from a broken pipe at the foundry was running across the road. Ibro's running rhythm would have led him straight into the water. He adjusted his steps and jumped over. The bag pulled him down. He lost his balance. Stayed on his feet with great difficulty. I thought I could see something small falling.

"Are you coming?" I shouted. Ibro was bent over looking for something on the ground.

"Fucking hell, I lost the dice!" he shouted and went on rummaging around like a chicken in the weak light of the streetlights.

Through my drunken brain a flash of recognition. History is a circle, not of people, but of events which are repeated over and over. What once Caesar did was now repeated by Ibro.

"Found them," reported Ibro, out of breath. We jumped on the bus. Sat on the front seats. The driver drove off. A fresh breeze pleasantly ruffled our hair. I was sitting next to Selim, squashed against the side of the bus. His shoulders took up a seat and a half.

Selim lifted the beer and me through the window of the dormitory.

The room seemed completely different. Ibro had covered

all the walls with pictures of naked women cut out from various magazines. I opened the window and pissed out. I didn't feel like sneaking to the toilet. Ibro and Selim did the same. We sat on the floor and threw the dice. At first we wrote down the points. Soon gave up. We drank and stacked the empty bottles into a pyramid.

We stopped throwing dice. Ibro and I smoked. Selim was sitting on his bed, rocking, pissed out of his head.

"We need music now," said Ibro.

On all fours he managed to get to the cassette player on the table. He looked through the cassettes, found the right one, and put it into the player. He turned the volume as high as it would go. He couldn't find enough strength to crawl back to the middle of the room where we were. He stayed lying next to the table with his back leaning on the wall under the window, singing the refrain loudly.

"I'LL GIVE YOU MY HEART!!!!"

I was watching him. He shouted, "You know who's singing?"

I tried to be nice and sociable.

"Christiaan Barnard?" I asked.

He probably didn't hear me. He said another name, which immediately escaped me.

"You know, I saw him. In person. Can you imagine? I wasn't more than a meter away from him. He sang and I stood in the first row. I could've touched him if I'd reached out. He who is in all the papers. I love him more than any other singer because he sings anywhere. In every village, even if there are only three houses. He's the only one of those who are on TV that you can go and see with your own eyes."

He's right. Those who parade on TV were rarely seen around here.

"Can you hear his singing? How can you not love him? I know, this is our music, not yours. You're always singing something in foreign languages. But still, you have to admit he's a wonderful singer."

I nodded. I was just about to open my mouth to tell him that in the shit of everyday existence, everybody buys what suits him most in the huge and diverse market of dreams. According to your own wishes, tastes, and means. With the feeling of guilt brought on by upbringing. It doesn't matter whether you're one of those who buy their escape from the everyday with a *shoobe-doobe-doo* or one of those who, with a superiority complex (from the same source), go for the to-be-or-not-to-be-that-is-the-question trip. It's all just dreams. But I didn't say anything. A feeling that it would be fruitless and pointless, along with the general impotence of words, choked the sentence in my throat.

Selim took a last gulp from the bottle and hurled it towards the table. He hit the cassette player and knocked it to the floor. The cassette started dragging. The tape got wrapped around the driving mechanism and tore. The music was finished.

Ibro asked, "What's the matter, you don't like it?"

I admired his talent for observation.

Selim got up slowly, to his best ability.

"Listen to me Ibro," he said, "you've covered all the walls with your naked women —" he pointed with a wave of his hand to the *corpus delicti* "— without asking me. All right. But we're roommates and half the walls are mine, half yours. Is that right?"

Ibro nodded.

"I'll divide it in half now. And that's how it stays."

He opened the wardrobe and started looking through the pockets on his working clothes. He pulled out a tape measure, went to the corner by the window, and said to me, "Hold it here, will you?"

I went over and held the start of the tape. We measured the wall. It went slowly. Mainly because of the tape, which kept slipping through my fingers and winding back into the box. Finally he decided where the middle was. I held my finger on the point he'd shown me. He again went to look in his pockets. He came back with a screwdriver and put it on the bed. He took the wardrobe door off its hinges and leaned it against the wall. With the screwdriver, he drew a line along the edge of the door. Some cunts and tits were split in two. He took the door back but couldn't put it back on its hinges however hard he tried. He gave up and just leaned it against the wardrobe.

"Ibro, now I'm going to take off everything from my half and give it to you. What you do on your half doesn't bother me. All right?"

"All right," said Ibro with candor.

"Fair?"

"Fair," confirmed the one sitting on the floor. It seemed he really did think so.

I helped Selim to pull the photographs from his part of the wall. He put the pile on the table. I leaned on the door and watched him. Ibro's head was hanging lower and lower on his chest. He was already asleep.

Selim unlocked his drawer and took out both posters. He unfolded them. I helped him stick them on the wall. There was a drop of dried blood on Nastassja's face on the poster for *Tess*. Carefully he tore out the pages with Nastassja from *Playboy* and stopped to think.

"Fuck the bastards," he sighed with anger. "They do this deliberately."

The bastards had put different pictures on both sides of each page. Two per sheet of paper. You couldn't stick one up without covering the other. I suggested an innovation.

"Stick it on with tape along the right-hand edge only. That way you'll be able to turn the page and see both pictures if you want."

He did as I suggested.

"What they wouldn't do to sell more. They make you buy at least two," he added, joining me. We stood staring at the photographs from three meters away.

The pages were sticking out from the wall.

With a small piece of tape, he stuck the top left corners, too. He left enough room to the right of each picture to turn it that way and stick it down again.

It looked a lot better now.

We stood there admiring the photos. Selim was completely engrossed. My attention was drawn to a picture of Nastassja's face. It reminded me of Ingrid Bergman, when she whispers that "Play it. . . ." A good scene. I adjusted my hat with my palm and moved my lips to shift the cigarette to the corner of my mouth.

Ibro was standing next to me, looking at me with surprise.

"What's the matter? Are you in pain?"

He made me feel embarrassed. I quickly moved my hand away from the imaginary hat and stopped twisting my lips with the imaginary cigarette.

"Give me a cigarette," I said sharply.

We lit up. Selim was still gaping at the wall, motionless. Ibro joined him.

He didn't need long for the final verdict. He asked, "What's wrong with this one? Did she forget to put on her ass and tits before filming?"

He laughed. He liked the joke. But only him. He found himself caught between two murderous looks. His laughter stuck in his throat.

"It's nothing, I was only joking," he said and went to the corner to mend the cassette. Selim went back to looking at Nastassja.

I drank another beer. The last one.

Ibro was asleep with the cassette player in his lap. I put the bottle on the top of the pyramid.

It fell down. The sound of the rolling bottles knocking against each other accompanied me down the corridor.

I didn't feel like jumping through the window. The warden

was asleep in his small room. Outside a warm spring breeze was blowing. The smell of sulfur was coming from the foundry.

I threw up leaning on the fence and stumbled home.

Tongues of flame shot up through the chimney.

CHAPTER 4

I was in my blue work suit again. I climbed over the foundry fence, landed clumsily, and stopped to brush the dust off my trousers. Young bodies spilled out of the secondary school across the road. I lit up, leaned on the inside of the fence, and waited.

Long Legs came past. Our eyes met. I'd noticed her for the first time half a year ago but never got any further than looking. There'd never been a real opportunity. She was nearly as tall as me, with long hair falling down her back. A girl for canoodling with on the sandy beaches of the Seychelles, wherever that may be.

I jumped, grabbed the top of the fence, and started climbing up the mesh.

"Hey you, stop!" somebody shouted right behind my back.

The guard.

I let go and fell back on his territory and with a sad look said goodbye to Long Legs, who was disappearing in the crowd. I ran off. The guard behind me. To my misfortune, he was without an arm.

Old age had slowed him down. What he lacked for in speed he made up for in stubbornness.

I zigzagged between heaps of scrap metal. I stopped now and again to wait.

He always showed up from behind a bend. A crane moved above my head. I threw myself to the ground. The metal spider's legs were a meter above my head. The operator blew his horn. Lying down lost me all my advantage over the guard.

I ran into a huge building, past a container with bubbling, steaming, thick fluid. And then into the next hall alongside the railway lines.

He followed me.

I ran straight into the heat. As if I'd hit a wall. I could hardly distinguish the figures of workers in protective clothing standing around the open door to the furnace. On the wall opposite there was a clothes hanger with some protective clothing next to a lonely picture of a naked woman and the names of two football clubs.

I wrapped a heavy asbestos coat around my shoulders and put on a hood that covered most of my face. For eyes there were two little windows made of darkened glass.

I looked around the hall. Somebody was poking the fire with a long metal stick. Two other workers were shoveling coke into the furnace. The fourth one was pushing a trolley along the narrow tracks. I helped him push. We tipped the trolley and emptied the contents into a heap. I turned away from the fire and lifted my hood. The guard was already in the hall. He turned right by the door and went up the metal stairs to the gallery, which ran along the whole wall to the stairs leading down to the exit. I pushed the hood back onto my face. We pushed the trolley to the two workers who started filling it with their shovels.

"Is that you Egon?" said my temporary co-worker and lifted his hat. It was Ibro.

I did the same. A quick look around. The guard wasn't there any more.

I took off the hood and put it under my arm.

"Hi Ibro. How did you recognize me?"

"I smelled you."

I hadn't had any Cartier on for two days now. The scent that had been absorbed into my skin must have been brought out by my sweat, which was flowing profusely. I was too used to the smell to notice it.

Ibro looked shocked.

"Do you work here, too?"

I grinned widely.

"No, oh no. Let's say I'm just passing through."

The trolley was full.

"Are you in a hurry?"

"No."

"Wait for me then. I'll just take this and then I can go and eat."

"Okay," I nodded.

He pushed the hood back onto his face and shoved at the trolley.

"I've got to tell you something," he added before he concentrated on flexing and torturing his muscles.

I stood by the exit and leaned on the fence along the stairs from the gallery.

The two who were filling the trolley put their shovels against the wall and left. Ibro was hanging his coat and hood on the hanger. I joined him and took off mine.

The cold outside made me shiver. I felt my back with my palm. My clothes were soaked.

Ibro offered me a cigarette and lit it with a match. He looked around as if to make sure there'd be no witnesses to our conversation.

"I've fallen in love," he said.

Damn the southerly wind, damn the spring. It'll fuck up each and every one of us.

"I saw her today. In the morning. When I was going to work."

In these situations I never know what sort of expression to put on my face. Even if I'd had a crocodile's face Ibro wouldn't have noticed it because of his enthusiasm.

"I already know her name!"

He leaned towards me and whispered, "Ajsha."

"Beautiful, yes," I said.

"A beautiful name, isn't it? If you could only see her. How beautiful she is."

I nodded.

The sweat drying on my back was making me feel colder and colder.

"You are going to the canteen, aren't you Ibro?"

"Yes."

"Me, too. Let's go."

We walked slowly towards the brick building. More and more people were going the same way.

"I'll point her out to you," he exclaimed enthusiastically. "You'll see, she's terribly beautiful. Even you'll have to admit it. You who knows everything about women."

I looked at him.

"Who told you that?"

He was embarrassed. He wasn't sure whether he'd said too much. He admitted.

"Selim."

He was looking at me with the eyes of a dog asking for forgiveness.

I nodded. It was all right. In the years of sitting quietly in the bar, alone with his beer, Selim must have seen me with many women. In many different circumstances.

We went into the canteen and lined up.

Ibro kept jumping up to look around. I felt very unpleasant.

He was like a pupil who was taking his teacher to see something he'd made and was impatiently anticipating his praise. A rebuke would break his heart. I decided to praise his chosen one without any reservations. If you try you can find something worth praising in every woman. White lies are like small, empty cushions. But lying down on them is still more comfortable than lying down without them. He started hitting me on the back as if he were trying to break into me.

"There! There she is. She's eating. Can you see?"

He pointed to the long rows of tables. Body after body. All in blue coats.

All similar faces. The ones coming and the ones going, all juggling with their trays. I couldn't see her.

"Can you see her?" he asked again.

"Yes, yes," I nodded and looked around more to please him than out of any real interest.

"She's a real beauty, isn't she?"

"Yes, yes," I kept nodding, still not seeing Ajsha.

The crowd moved, and for a moment I caught a glimpse of the girl I'd flirted with the day before. The one from the nail-packing department. She noticed me, too. We smiled at each other. I fell into her eyes.

Other people hid her again.

I became aware of Ibro trembling as if he was just about to throw all his clothes off.

He turned towards me and grabbed me by the collar. Shook me.

"Did you see? Did you see that!?"

I didn't get it.

"How she smiled at me," he finished his sentence.

Ooooooh, damn spring. Damn shit.

Ibro's face was radiant. Shining like the sun. He was floating. He put his arm around my shoulder and whispered in my ear, "You see, I've got every chance. . . ."

I didn't know what to say, what to do with myself.

"Yes, yes. . . ." I mumbled.

There's no greater confidence than that brought on by the smile of a beautiful woman. Ibro suddenly seemed taller.

"Tell me honestly. Is she beautiful or not?"

"She's beautiful," I admitted.

"Like a picture?"

"Like a picture."

A new admission.

"Have you ever seen eyes like that? Eyes so deep you could drown in them?"

I agreed. With all my heart.

And felt more and more awkward.

At last it was our turn to get the broth with ribs. I got three portions and a kilo of bread.

Ibro was surprised.

"How can you eat so much and not put weight on? You're as thin as a skeleton."

I smiled and waited with the answer until we sat down. Ibro tried to push nearer to Ajsha without success. The only two empty chairs were right at the other end, next to the counter. I broke the end off the bread loaf and started chewing it. I took the ribs out of the broth, shook off the sauce, and wrapped the ribs in paper napkins. Then I put them together with the bread into a plastic bag I had brought with me.

Ibro was looking at the three bowls and the bag. I explained before he asked.

"It's not for me. I've got a friend who doesn't eat anything. Unless people bring him something. When he's by himself he just forgets about food. Because people visit him rarely he doesn't often get to eat. I'm going to see him tonight."

He looked at me to see if I was serious and then he mumbled, "Whatever next."

He pulled the ribs out of his broth, wrapped them, and gave them to me. He was a good soul. I was even more embarrassed.

I offered him the three bowls of broth.

"Have these if you want."

"Don't you want them?"

"No."

He pulled the bowls towards him and started to spoon up the food.

"The work made me very hungry. It was grueling."

"Yeah," I said emphatically and nodded.

"At least I'll sleep well," he added.

The type who always finds something positive in everything. An incorrigible optimist. Nothing can screw up a person like that apart from a woman. Probably. I didn't know him enough to be able to determine that yet.

Suddenly he stopped eating. He looked towards the wall on the right and beamed a terrible smile with his whole mouth towards Ajsha, who had just pushed her tray through the hatch and was leaving the canteen. She was looking in our direction. I smiled at her.

She returned the smile.

"Ooooooh," sighed Ibro. Three beans flew out of his mouth and rolled on the table. Ajsha had gone. I concentrated on chewing the bread crust. Ibro twisted in his chair and couldn't take his eyes off her.

"What's the matter Ibro? Did this one forget to put on her ass and tits before she went to work, too?"

I really shouldn't have talked about her behind. The loose coat didn't show any more than the fact that it couldn't have been disproportionately large. And you could only imagine her breasts under the heavy material.

He blushed and started fidgeting.

"I was only joking. I didn't mean to hurt anyone."

I nodded understandingly.

"I was only joking, too."

He couldn't eat any more. He was looking towards the door through which his beloved had left.

"Let's go!" I said.

I pushed the bread in my pocket.

We took the trays back and went out.

She was leaning on the fence, warming herself in the sun. She undid her coat. She was wearing jeans and a gray blouse with a barely visible floral pattern. It didn't look bad. She was that type of woman. With a wonderful figure. Ibro was whining. I stopped at the other end of the yard, and he was forced to stay with me. We lit up. Ajsha pulled a cigarette out of the packet and held it unlit between her fingers. I went over and offered her a light. She thanked me.

"It's your turn again tomorrow."

She laughed. A beautiful laugh, just a trifle loud and hollow.

"Which department do you work in?" she asked.

"Nowhere. I just come here to eat."

She didn't understand.

"I get free vouchers from some acquaintances. When I'm hungry I put on borrowed work clothes and come to eat."

Laughter again.

"I thought I hadn't seen you before. I noticed you straight away yesterday."

It was said as a fact, not a compliment.

She went on.

"You know, I look at a man's shoes first."

"His shoes?!"

It was my turn not to understand and to laugh.

"Yes, his shoes. Look!"

I looked at my tennis shoes, tied with scraps of shoelaces. Then I looked around and saw only winkle-pickers with raised heels clunking everywhere.

"When I see footwear like that, it's a real turn off. I don't bother looking at anything else," she said.

I looked at Ibro's feet. Winkle-pickers with raised heels.

We chatted until she looked at her watch and said she had to go back to work. I went back to Ibro. He was all eyes.

"What did she say?" he pounced.

"We chatted a bit, about shoes."

"Shoes? You start a conversation with an unknown woman talking about shoes?!"

"Not me, her."

"And what did you say about me? I saw you looking at me."

"She likes your shoes."

"Oh, these are nothing. You just see the shoes and clothes I'm going to get when I get my first paycheck."

I knew precisely what he'd get. I said goodbye and left. He had to return to his trolley, too. I walked towards my flat through the foundry. In a tangle of huge pipes beneath the hot air stoves sat Selim. He looked deep in thought. I wanted to go past unnoticed, but he saw me and called to me. I said hello.

Whenever I talked to Selim I always had an unpleasant feeling that repelled and attracted me at the same time. Somewhere under the deep layers of material, a knife was hiding. It was edging out through his eyes. I always look at a person's eyes first. They determine whether I'll get to the shoes at all.

Selim was a ponderer. Somebody who doesn't talk much, who's always chewing something in his head and from time to time surprises those around him with a birth. And an occasional abortion, of course. Or a birth to something deformed. I sat next to him. The hot pipe warmed my ass.

"I'm going," Selim said, "today after work."

"Where?"

"To Italy."

"To get some jeans?"

He looked at me as if I was an idiot.

"To Rome."

"Are you going to change your religion?"

The same look again. I decided to drop the sarcasm and let him finish.

"I'm going to Nastassja's," he said.

"Is she in Rome?"

"Yes, I went to the hairdresser's today. To have my hair cut."

His hair really was a bit shorter.

I couldn't see the connection.

I waited for the explanation.

"They've got some German magazines there. I saw her picture in one of them. Rome was mentioned a few times."

He pulled a page torn from a magazine and gave it to me.

"Can you translate it please?" he asked me.

I read it.

Gave him a short summary of the gossip.

"She's living with her new man in a rented apartment in Rome."

Selim nodded.

"That's where I'm going."

We were silent for a few minutes.

"Selim, listen. There's a million guys like you out there. You won't be able to even look in through the fence and the bodyguards. They'll smash you up however strong you are. And who do you think you are? A nothing and nobody. In Rome even more than here. Even if Nastassja was in a very generous mood you'd only get her autograph, maybe an original or maybe just a copy, from her PR. Are you sure you really want her signature? If it were on a check, I'd take it. Now think about it."

Selim nodded.

"You're right. Nothing and nobody," he repeated and again drowned in his own thoughts. I lit a cigarette and finished it.

He was sitting next to me motionless. My ass was boiling hot.

Quietly, I said goodbye. I didn't want to disturb his thoughts.

He didn't say anything, probably hadn't even heard me. He was staring in front of him.

I left. I thought I could hear his voice behind me repeating, ""Nothing and nobody . . ."

I looked back. I couldn't see him any more, he was hidden by the pipes. A white cloud of steam whooshed out of a valve.

I jumped over the fence and ran across the road. Magda came from the opposite direction, holding hands with some guy. I'd never seen him before.

I couldn't decide whether to say hello or not. Maybe I shouldn't show that we knew each other.

I waited. She smiled and waved to me. We said hello. Went our separate ways.

I took a shower and went to sleep. I hung the plastic bag with the ribs on the window handle.

I got up, had another shower, put the working clothes in the wardrobe, and left for Karla's.

I rang the bell once. Twice. Nothing could be heard in the flat. I was just about to go when a shadow appeared in the peephole. The door opened. I'd woken her up. Wrapped in a dressing gown, she looked at me sleepily, as if she was seeing me for the first time.

Finally she smiled.

"Come in."

She moved away to make room for me.

I went in, took off my jacket and my shoes.

"Are you happy with the sewing work?" she asked. I wasn't quite sure whether there wasn't a hint of ridicule in her voice.

"Yes, beautiful work. Is he a tailor?"

"Something like that." Ridicule again.

I wanted to put my arms around her.

Gently but firmly she pushed me away.

"Wait till I've had a shower and woken up a bit. Would you make me some coffee?"

I lit the gas ring and put on some water. I could hear the splashing of the shower from the bathroom.

I made the coffee and filled her cup. The rest was for me. I diluted it with milk and sat down. Pulled a piece of bread from my pocket and ate it.

The cup of coffee opposite was slowly getting cold.

The shower went quiet.

I took the cup and, balancing it so that the black liquid didn't spill, went to the bathroom.

Karla was standing naked in front of the mirror, combing her wet shoulder-length hair.

"I brought your coffee before it gets completely cold," I explained my entry, standing in the door.

She turned around and said firmly, "No, I don't want it."

We started laughing simultaneously.

I quickly put the cup on the washing machine so as not to spill it.

We were looking at each other relishing the laughter.

She took a long sip of coffee and went back to combing her hair.

I leaned on the wall, watching her. When she put down the brush and walked past me, I reached out with my right hand and caught her. She didn't resist.

"When's the alarm going off today?" I asked.

A deadly invention. It must have destroyed more lives than a machine gun.

"At seven. I've been invited out for dinner."

"With a fine gentleman in the prime of his years?"

She nodded.

She took the empty cups and saucers to the sink. I followed her and put my arms around her. She turned around in my arms and kissed me.

"And what happened to your trademark?" she asked.

"Yeah, Cartier is gone. I'm working hard to get a new one."

"Of course, you'll succeed," she added ironically.

I didn't think it was worth nodding. I pulled the belt that held her robe together and put my palm on her skin, hot from the water.

"Do you want me?"

"No."

She looked at me with surprise.

My finger was playing with her nipple.

"What do you want then?" she asked.

"Don't know. I'm tired. Fed up. Depressed by the pointlessness of it all."

She nodded.

"I know the feeling. Very well. . . ."

"I know."

We stopped talking. It seemed to me that the silence was pushing us down.

Karla probably felt uneasy, too. She started talking with an unusually cheerful voice, which sounded grotesque, artificial, and affected. But then I realized that she always talked like that, I just hadn't noticed it until now.

"What's the matter," she said, "you big lover? Are you going to tell me one of your little stories in which you're always the main hero and the winner?"

"I won't. Don't worry. But as for these stories, we're all always winners. A pensioner tells her friends in great detail how she told off the butcher who was just about to give her some meat full of gristle. At the same moment the butcher is telling everybody how he'd foisted meat soaked in water to make it heavier on some old bat. That's the way it goes."

"I know."

We went quiet again. Deep in thought, I ran my thumb around the base of her breast.

"Okay," she said. "Tell me what's bothering you. Every day I hear at least one sad story, usually in the evening. Let's say I'm working overtime without getting paid. Everybody says that psychiatrists have replaced priests and confessionals, but nobody mentions whores, who work a lot harder than any of them."

I grinned.

"Tell me now. Is it a woman?"

"No, not at all. This time I really haven't got any problems with women."

"Haven't there been any women fainting in the street at the sight of you walking towards them?"

Her cynicism didn't bother me. Most of my own utterances came from the same domain.

"You know very well I'm not one of those men who girls sigh over when they're coming towards them in the street."

She lifted her eyebrow questioningly without opening her mouth.

I continued, "They sigh over me when I'm walking away from them."

She laughed.

"I didn't know that detectives from black-and-white movies were still riding around."

I shrugged my shoulders.

"Fuck it, watching films helped me experience the world, wherever that may be."

"But you won't tell me a sad story?"

"You won't get away without it, don't worry. Tactically speaking, strategic operations are in process, which will get me a new bottle of perfume. I won't tell you the names of the victims, but one Selim happened to come by —"

She interrupted me. "A hero of labor?"

"Yes, but somehow not through his own fault. . . . Anyway, this Selim is heading for ruin. He doesn't mean anything to me, you understand, but his cracking and breaking reverberates in me like a distant memory. He's going through the same shit that I went through. It's clear how it'll end. I don't want to be there. . . ."

"Go away."

"I've already told you I'm just finishing the Cartier project. I can't go anywhere yet, at least for a while."

"Oh you young businessmen. Meetings and business are all that you think about."

"Young, urban, professional," I mumbled.

"Exactly," she announced ceremoniously.

I moved away to the window to look at the foundry and then through the bedroom door. I reached out and stroked the spines of the books on the bookcase.

Karla was watching me from the door.

The atmosphere was still heavy, pregnant with sadness.

"You have studied many things," I said, "and finished a degree or two in the process."

"And all that while I was working as well."

"While you were fucking," I corrected her immediately, as always concerned about the clarity of expression.

She nodded smilingly.

"I searched for it first in books then in men. Now I'm not searching anymore."

"Try traveling. That's the essence of everything."

"I'll think about it. Even though this advice failed with you."

"Yes, but it was wonderful nonetheless."

I turned to the books again.

"Stop looking," she said. "You've already taken everything that could interest you."

"I only borrowed them. Indefinitely. And there weren't that many books to make it worth getting worked up about. Two or three."

"Sixteen."

"Well, maybe. But the only one I'm using is *Summa Theologica*."

"I've never quite understood your fascination with Thomas Aquinas."

"Listen now. I'm going to use one of those insipid, meaningless phrases they use in encyclopedias for nearly every famous person. Are you ready?"

"Say it."

"He was seven centuries ahead of his time."

She looked at me questioningly.

"I'll tell you a story."

"You're always telling those."

"At least you're used to them. Anyway, Aquinas was a real Dominican, a soldier of God. He traveled to all the colleges and universities of Europe, which was the world then, lecturing, writing, and thinking. Heresies blossomed so quickly they couldn't even count them. But Aquinas immediately fought each one of them with his logic. They invited him to lecture in Italy. They went to Mass one Sunday. While singing 'Don't leave us when we lose the strength to carry on,' he sat down and stopped. Everything. He stopped writing, he stopped lecturing, he stopped eating. Nothing. His secretary asked him how he could just leave his work unfinished and he answered, 'I can't go on anymore. Everything I have written is meaningless.' There."

"A nice story, better than usual. But I still don't get why Thomas was seven centuries ahead of his time."

"Faith was still strong then. In those days they believed in God, later on in reason, and finally in changing the world. Revolution. A paradise on earth. The Party. Now faith is dead. If you've got any sense at all you can't believe in anything anymore, least of all in reason. Everything people have been fighting for all these centuries is garbage. Nothing. Everything's been spoiled. Even I've started to philosophize instead of chasing young girls, which goes to prove that you can't rely on anything and anybody anymore."

We were silent.

"Karla, you make me talk nonsense sometimes. It's best if I leave. I'll go and work on that perfume, seduce a few girls.

Anything is better than sitting waiting for death. I'm not Niempsch."

"Who?"

"Another story. Next time."

I went to the kitchen.

"Stay a bit longer," she said.

I looked at her. She suddenly seemed fragile and vulnerable. We used to live together years ago. It lasted a few months. The cynical, unattainable Karla changed from a femme fatale to a vulnerable person without any support. She wanted to lean on the cynical and unattainable Egon, as if she hadn't noticed that he was no longer a macho man but a dangling man. We were too alike. We could act for a few hours a week but not for twenty-four hours a day. We brought each other down. I packed and went away, and when I called in again after a month, we'd both managed to mend our masks. But we never discussed trying to live together again. Not a word.

"I'm going," I said.

She was probably thinking similar thoughts and chewing over the same memories.

"All right," she said. "I wasn't thinking when I invited you. A moment of weakness."

Why flog a dead horse?

I stepped through the door and firmly decided not to look back.

I was at the end of the corridor. I still hadn't heard the sound of the door closing.

"Egon."

She called me. With a sad and lonely undertone.

I turned around.

"Come back for another kiss," she said.

I did as asked.

It lasted a long time and as usual, it was I who stopped it.

"I'm going, Karla." I stroked her cheek with the knuckles of my fist.

She nodded.

"Bye, Egon."

"Bye," I repeated.

I couldn't get rid of the feeling that I was really saying goodbye.

I ran to the stairs, pressed my feet together, and slid down the solid concrete edge like it was a playground slide. It's possible if your feet are big enough.

I looked back once. Karla was looking after me.

The alarm behind her back went off.

I stood in front of the main entrance wondering where to go. I scratched my cheeks and decided to have a shave. I went to the flat and changed my mind. I wasn't in the right mood for that. If I hadn't shaved for a fortnight I could last another week or so.

I took the bag with the ribs and the bread and went to the bar.

The pensioners were sitting at a table. "A red hot poker up their ass," one of them was just saying.

It was too early to go to Noodle's. It had only just gotten dark.

I went wandering around the town.

Selim stood in front of the cinema. Clean shaven, in a white velvet suit, a white shirt, a black bow tie, and a carnation in his buttonhole. A few meters away from him stood a group of his comrades from the dormitory. They were sniggering. He paid no attention to them.

I strode over to him and said hello.

"Do you have a date?"

"Yes, I'm going to the cinema," he said.

I didn't have to ask which film was showing. Nastassja was looking at me from the display case with her catlike eyes.

"Are you coming?" he invited.

I went.

We sat in the back row. There were about twenty other people in the auditorium besides us.

The lights went off. Selim went completely still. I swung my legs over the back of the seats in front of me and cradled the bag of ribs.

The audience was split into three groups, like little islands in the auditorium. They were rustling candy wrappers. They were shouting comments. Competing with witticisms.

After less than five minutes the film broke. The auditorium was full of whistling. The lights came on.

Selim got up and walked through the whole auditorium to the platform in front of the screen.

He stood silently in the middle of the stage.

Slowly they all went quiet, asking themselves what he was up to and expecting some juicy jokes.

He spoke.

"If anybody opens their mouth or makes any noise whatsoever during the rest of this film, I'll smash their face in."

The three in the first row laughed loudly.

Selim went down the stairs, walked up to them, and smashed their faces in.

Then he went back on the stage.

There was a deadly silence in the auditorium.

He looked up to the projection room and shouted, "And if the film breaks once more, I'll smash your face in."

Everything was quiet up there, too.

Selim returned to his seat and sat motionless.

The film didn't break anymore. We watched it in fear-induced silence right to the end.

When the lights came on again, I could hardly get up. Both my legs had gone to sleep. My ass was full of pins and needles. My back hurt.

I hadn't dared to move for two hours because the rickety rows of wooden chairs accompanied every little move with a sad creaking.

Selim went to see the next performance, too.

I was very glad to be rid of his company. His madness was growing by the minute. And I had no idea where, when, and how it would all stop.

I became scared.

I set off for Noodle's. He lived in an old bunker from the Second World War, high above the town, in the middle of the woods. A few years ago the police used to amuse themselves by parking their cars in front of the entrance to the bar just before closing time and picking up all their old acquaintances who were sitting at the tables, me included. They drove us far up into the hills and let us out in the middle of the woods. They wished us a good journey and drove off. It was dawn the next day by the time we wandered back into the valley, scratched, bruised, frozen, and grubby. They repeated this throughout the summer, at least once a week. Occasionally they'd leave one of us sitting at the table, but it was never Noodle. He always took part in the transportation until he got fed up and after one of the rides stayed in the hills. Didn't come back. The wisest one gives in.

Once every two months he'd call in the valley, come for a short visit. Sitting in the bar he cursed the world and did what he got his nickname for: he cut thin noodles of his skin from his arm or leg with a razor blade.

I was already across the river at the other side of the foundry. I cut through the rubble of the abandoned workrooms, avoiding the sheets of corrugated iron that had fallen from the roofs.

The sky was full of stars. A gentle, warm breeze was peeling a thick blanket of red dust from the walls.

I stopped in a bar, an island of light and singing in the midst of the rubble. It must have been in the center of the foundry once, but then the foundry moved and left it to the slow decay and the faithful customers. A few years ago, I used to like coming here for a beer. I was attracted by the magical and romantic interior. After three crumbling stairs you'd get to a dark corridor with creaking floorboards. The entrance was on the left. A brass door handle, very heavy under your hand. There were gaps between the door and the frame. Through a gap in the upper right corner a ray of light escaped. After it a thin wreath of cigarette smoke. You'd go in, and the first thing you'd notice was a bare, weak bulb at the end of the wires sticking out from the ceiling. The circle of light from it only reached a part of the bar on the left and a couple of tables. The rest was in darkness.

When your eyes got used to the dark, they met the eyes of the small, hunchbacked waitress, a very old woman. A tuft of hair grew out of a mole on her nose. She waited for your order silently. You paid for your beer and sat down. The other customers, hidden by darkness, only then continued their conversations. Old drunks, in tatty clothes, usually without an arm or a leg. There were no accidental customers here. Only regulars. The bar was never mentioned in the crime reports of the newspaper anymore. A few times I'd witnessed a brawl. Knives shone. Nobody called the police. They took care of their own business among themselves. You drank your beer, inhaling your surroundings. Magical.

I felt like Oliver Twist.

I didn't know who or why anybody thought it worthwhile investing money in this ruin. Instead of the light bulb, a long neon light stretched across the ceiling. The wooden bar had been replaced by a heap of glass and plastic. The peepholes were enlarged into windows. They'd fucked it all up. The charming waitress had turned into an ordinary old woman. She didn't even have a hunchback anymore, and she was only slightly bent. She blinked in the neon light along with the customers, whose appearance had changed from vicious crooks to ordinary workers. I never went there anymore.

I avoided it this time, too. Sad because of progress, which spoils every trace of homeliness.

I had already reached the ghetto. The place which officially wasn't there and which the majority of people on the right bank of the river didn't even know existed. Or so they claimed. Long rows of huts built of planks of wood, wooden beams, and corrugated cardboard leaning on the slope. Full of workers from the south waiting to get a job at the foundry. If they got one a flat soon followed. They moved to the right bank into a more modern ghetto.

I walked right by the windows. I cut across the beams of light coming from them. Cassette players and children were screaming. The warm wind carried with it the smell of shit and old piss. I peered through a window. Somebody was trying to move a horse to the other end of the room by kicking it so that he could see the television.

Something has to be said here. Loudly and clearly. Here it goes:

THIS ISN'T POVERTY, THIS IS A WAY OF LIFE.

People can make their beds the way they happen to like them. At least within their means. If you've managed to build a hut, you could manage to build a stable, too. I knew quite a few who didn't want to move to the right bank at all. And others who did move but who kept pigs in their bathroom, ripped the parquet floor out of their bedrooms and grew tomatoes instead. Apparently they grew very well. On Sundays the fire brigade would drive around the town, putting out barbecues lit in the kitchens, on balconies, or in the cellars.

IT'S A WAY OF LIFE.

So there.

The ghetto was behind me, and I started going up the slope. A well-trodden path zigzagged among the bushes. All the holes and bumps were illuminated by the large, pale moon. I stopped and listened. In front of me I could distinguish a long, tall building. It probably used to be a military warehouse. Now it was fully inhabited. I squatted behind a bush and had a good look around. The hairs on my back stood up with fear. Maybe this time I'd manage to get past without it noticing me. I moved forward on the balls of my feet. I turned swiftly. There was nobody behind me. The shadows seemed impenetrably dense. Suddenly I felt like running. I managed to get a grip on myself. In spite of the creature that appeared every time I went past there, my fear was completely groundless. And because of that even stronger.

I turned off the path onto the grass.

Going right into the woods to avoid the building.

I stopped and looked back.

Nobody.

My neck was tingling like mad now.

I took a deep breath. I tried to get used to the creature's sound that would cut through the silence.

I had taken three steps when I heard it right behind me.

OOOOOOOOOOₒₒₒₒₒₒₒₒₒOOOOOOOOOOOOO

I didn't have to turn around. I knew who was howling. I wanted to run up into the hill as usual but stopped and turned around. I don't know why. One of those nights maybe.

The creature stood two meters behind me.

It didn't stop howling.

I'd never heard anything like it before. It sounded like a dog howling at the moon but it was full of terror, sad and lonely.

And it came from a human throat.

I could hardly stop shaking. Another impulse to escape. To run away from the sound that was tearing my brain apart.

And it wasn't loud at all.

For the first time I looked at the howling figure for more than a second.

It seemed to be a woman of indeterminate age. You could hardly make out her eyes. Her nose and mouth were pushed to the left. They'd been forced sideways by a huge lump, which swelled up the right side of the face. It was red, soft, and porous, with white spots, like mold. Eczema maybe. The whole face was completely red. On top of her head was straight thin hair, cut in a straight line. Her bony little figure gave the impression of a young girl. I thought I could see two small breasts under the tatty turtleneck.

She howled again.

OOOOOOOOOOooooooooooOOOOOOOOOOOOO

Everybody's got somebody who's a bigger victim than them. The lowest of the low. She was the scum of this pond. She walked around, accompanied by a flock of children, by cursing and stone throwing. A scene in slow motion floated in front of my eyes: I'm watching. She's standing on a concrete wall between the huts, howling. One of the children throws a stone. One that's almost too big for a child's hands. The stone flies towards her head. It hits the mark. In the middle of her lump. I'm waiting for it to squash like a tomato. But it doesn't. She's bleeding. She's lying on the floor howling. The lump remains whole. It's probably harder than it looks.

OOOOOOOOOOooooooooooOOOOOOOOOOOOO

I'd known about quite a few mentally ill women. The most-wanted were those who were mute as well. They'd get raped as soon they showed themselves in the street in the evenings.

Nobody touched this one probably. At least I couldn't imagine it. They even beat her with a stick to avoid touching her.

She howled again. Very quietly.

I spoke. Slowly, in a deep voice, articulating clearly.

"Hey, calm down, I won't hurt you."

I didn't even know if she was capable of understanding. It seemed to me that she liked it if somebody talked to her.

"I won't hit you, you know."

I shook my head.

"No, I won't."

She was watching me silently.

"The night is for sleeping, you know."

Below us a drunk shouted.

"Go home, go to bed. I'll walk you there."

I reached with my hand. I couldn't believe it. I watched the tips of the middle three fingers touching her shirt. No slime. The synthetic material under my fingers and the warmth of the body under it.

I took one step forward, towards the warehouse.

She followed.

We walked on the grass side by side. The dew sparkled on my shoes. All the way I was touching her with the balls of my fingers.

Repeating slowly as if I was lulling her to sleep, "Go to bed . . . everything's all right . . . go to bed . . ."

We came to the door.

She opened it and went in.

"I'm going now . . . sleep well . . ."

I stepped back on the grass. She was looking at me.

I gestured her inside with a wave of my palm.

"Go . . . everything's fine . . . sleep well."

The door closed.

I ran. In the woods, I tripped over a tree root sticking out of the ground and bumped into the trunk. My right arm was still stretched out.

I rubbed the fingers that had touched her against the trunk of a pine tree until my skin started stinging.

The foundry looked like a shiny snake in the valley below.

I sat down and lit up.

After the cigarette, I started climbing the hill. I had to rest frequently. My lungs were letting me down. Too many cigarettes.

At a certain height I again started tiptoeing. I was hoping that the wind wouldn't carry my scent to the hollow on the slope where they used to dig for gravel and that the dog wouldn't smell me. A Gypsy family lived there. For many years they used to live in a ramshackle old bus, which somebody had left at the abandoned gravel pit, I don't know why or how. One evening

I saw the glow of a fire as I walked past. I sat down next to the family as they stoically watched the bus burn. It burned fiercely, as if petrol had been poured on it. We lit up. I asked them why they didn't call the fire brigade. They looked at me as if I was an idiot. Slowly, as if to a child who hasn't quite grasped the finer points of life yet, they explained that it was the fire brigade who had set fire to the wreckage because it was illegal to live in an abandoned bus. Okay. From then on they lived in a tent next to the burnt frame. They tied their dog to the supporting pole of the small tent in the evenings. Whenever I went past, he smelled me and started barking and pulling at his chain. The tent collapsed.

It happened this time, too. The barking of the dog was joined by the cursing of the kicking inhabitants of the tent.

I ran past as fast as my lungs let me. The foundry was already considerably smaller behind me. The barking could hardly be heard. Then it changed to whimpering.

Somebody was beating him.

I carried on to Noodle's abode. It took me some time to find the entrance to the bunker, half buried in the ground, overgrown with ferns and bushes.

I went in.

In the middle of the round room, a candle shone. Noodle was lying on some cardboard with his back against the wall, staring in front of him.

I put the bag under my ass and sat next to the candle. I had to shift a few times before I could get my balance, sitting on the ribs.

I smoked a cigarette and started coughing. Thick phlegm came from my chest.

I stepped to the loophole and spat out.

Noodle noticed me at last.

"Oh, look who's here. Hi."

I threw the bag in front of him.

"I brought you some food."

He shook the contents onto the floor and looked at me gratefully.

I sat down on a piece of cardboard.

I was going to lean on my hands, but I changed my mind before I put them down. Everywhere there were small, black turds, dried out. Probably not Noodle's. They looked too old.

I went out to take a piss. When I got back, Noodle had already started gnawing the bones and tearing the bread.

"Here, have some," he offered.

I declined the meat. I slowly chewed a handful of bread.

Noodle filled his shrunken stomach as best he could. The leftovers he put on a heap of paper next to him. He fumbled through the cardboard. He rolled away a rusted helmet, with a hole in the side, and took out a thin book and offered me it.

"Here, you read things like this."

I took it, bent over the candle, and leafed through it. It was a very old Serbian edition of Rimbaud's poems. Pocket size, with a red cloth cover. Only the name of the author in the middle. It said REMBO, spelled out phonetically, in Serbian script. In the corner was Noodle's greasy thumb print.

I put the booklet in my breast pocket.

"Where did you get it?"

"I too sometimes take a walk through the scrap paper warehouse."

Indeed, there were heaps of old newspapers next to the bunker wall. Useful for many things. For cigarette rolling, for a blanket, a hat, for ass wiping, apparently you can even read them.

He pulled out a crumpled matchbox. He tore a piece of newspaper, shook some green bits from the box onto it, and rolled a joint. He made a mouthpiece from the bottom of the matchbox.

He lit it and took a puff.

Silently we passed the joint to each other.

I interrupted the silence.

"It's a good one. Is it from Hippy's plantation?"

"Yes, his seeds are by far the best."

Noodle often wandered around the woods and knew the area well. That's exactly why I'd come to him.

I started, "I'd like to ask you something."

He nodded. There's no visit without a reason.

"Where are Alfred's plantations?"

Even I knew where Hippy's was. But Alfred was more of a conspiratorial type.

Noodle told me the way to Alfred's bliss in this life without hesitation.

"Fuck it, that's life," he sighed at the end. More to himself.

I looked at him carefully to see if he wasn't getting one of his attacks.

He didn't seem to be. He put the joint out against the sole of his boot. He made another one, which traveled between us.

He leaned back and closed his eyes. I smoked to the end. I thought he was asleep.

I got up quietly, covered him with an opened newspaper, and went. When I got to the door, I could hear him behind me, "Thanks for the food."

I looked back.

"That's okay."

He was sitting motionless with his eyes closed.

I waited for my eyes to get used to the moonlight. As I set off, I could still see the flickering flame of the candle in front of my eyes.

The night was fresh, but not cold. The moonlight distorted trees into shapes unknown to me. I didn't feel comfortable. I'm a city child. Neon lights and dumpsters are my type of exterior.

On my right the dog barked. The sound of the collapsing tent mixed in with the cursing in all known languages. I ran.

The ghetto was dark and silent. I ran through it without looking back.

Higher up the barking turned to whimpering.

Somebody was beating the animal.

The foundry lights were coming nearer.

CHAPTER 5

I still hadn't shaved. I preferred to squeeze the Cartier bottle. But it was dead. Empty. I remembered Ajsha. I went outside. I stopped in front of the block of flats where Alfred lived. I opened the main door and climbed to the third floor to see if he was at home. He worked in the rolling-mill, which, with his education, he didn't have to do. He explained to his listeners that working there was a penance, the suffering that cleansed him.

Shit.

Local Jesuses are terribly unpleasant.

I listened at the door. One of those long-winded Pink Floyd numbers from their most nirvanistic period could be heard from the flat. I grinned like a pig.

I leaned on the banister and lit up. I took slow puffs, waited and laughed.

I put the cigarette out on a metal plate on the banister. Sparks fell down into the darkness.

The music was getting louder and louder. The male choir was singing a high *AAAAA AAAAA AAAAA*. Timpani struck. The right moment to go in had arrived.

The door was locked of course. I looked through my pockets, found a rusty nail, pushed it in the lock, and unlocked the door. I crossed the hall quietly and put my hand on the bedroom door handle. The music reached its peak. The voices in the choir had crashed apart and joined again to the rhythmic sound of the organ.

I opened the door.

"Hi, Alfred!" I shouted from the door, terribly glad to see him.

"I rang the bell. Nobody answered, probably because of the loud music. I tried the handle and it was unlocked."

The scene was what I expected and wanted it to be.

Alfred was sitting on the floor with his back against the bed. There was a female figure in a colorful cotton Indian dress and with very blond hair between us, obstructing my view of him.

The girl jumped up. She didn't look in my direction. She ran into the corner and leaned on the window, as if something terribly interesting was happening outside.

Alfred was trying to quickly do up his fly.

"If I'd known you weren't on your own I wouldn't have come in at all," I tried to comfort him.

He forgot to say hello, he was so busy with his zipper.

I stepped over to him and tapped his shoulder.

"Well, what's happened has happened."

He nodded and mumbled something. He looked me in the eyes. At least he wanted to. But to look up at someone from a half-lying position is very awkward. You feel inferior. He got up quickly.

His cheeks were still red.

"Hello," he said at last.

I nodded to him pleasantly and turned to the girl, who was still gazing through the window. An ear was sticking out from her hair. It was bright red.

I stepped forward and, with my leg in the air, noticed stains on the carpet and stepped over them jerkily.

"Alfred, you dripped something on the floor."

I bent over to have a closer look.

"Some fat or something like that."

Alfred couldn't collect himself at all. He kept looking at the girl. She stayed motionless. Only her ears were getting redder and redder.

"No," he said, "I've just had coffee with cream. I spilled a little."

He took a handkerchief from his pocket and started to wipe the carpet.

Alfred was a fox and a half. He did certain things in his own way. He chased young girls at Sunday school or in church, took them to his flat, excited them with his words and hands until they were beside themselves. Suddenly he stopped the petting and started talking about the sin of fucking before marriage. He let them stew in their red hot bodies before taking them in hand. Or, to be more accurate, before they took him in hand.

He always put the same record on, laid back on the carpet, and enjoyed it. I was looking at him with my back turned to the wardrobe. He was rubbing the stains with an expression of terrible disgust. He finished and held the handkerchief between two fingers, stretching his arm out in front of him, excused himself saying he'd be back in a second and went to the bathroom.

I decided to walk around the room and have a look around.

The girl gave no signs of life. Three walls were covered with a long line of still-lifes in varnished wooden frames, and the fourth wall had a bookcase along it.

Photographs of lonely trees. Streams running through the morning mist.

Pastoral idylls.

Last time I was here, not in the same circumstances, a row of images of saints, the Virgin Mary, Jesus, and God hung on all three walls.

I thought about how much effort must go into taking all the saints off the wall and replacing them with the pastoral before every hand-jerking session, and then restoring the room to its former look.

I went over to a photograph of a lonely baobab above which the savannah sun was setting and turned it around. The pope was giving me his blessing with his arms wide open. I nodded to him in a friendly way and pressed him back against the flowery-patterned wall.

If an earthquake should ever destroy this building, only these well-blessed bricks are going to remain in one piece. Amen.

I took a peep at the other side of a baby deer drinking from a stream, only to see the Virgin Mary with her baby in her lap.

I concentrated on the books. One long row of cheap religious crap. In the middle of the shelf stood a box of Cuban cigars, leaning on the spines of the books. I opened it, took out one cigar, sniffed it, and put it in my pocket. Running water could be heard from the bathroom.

Reading the book titles brought me right next to the girl.

I looked at her. She was quite tall, quite a bit taller than Alfred.

I went over to her right side and leaned my cheek on the windowpane. She wore large, horn-rimmed glasses. Slowly, taking pleasure in my impudence, I studied her face. She didn't even twitch.

Neither beautiful nor ugly, conditionally interesting. Middle-sized breasts with upturned nipples. Between the breasts a metal pendant of a dove in a shape of a cross. I bent down towards her hair and took in a deliberately noisy breath. She smelled of shampoo. Birch tree. She was dying with embarrassment. I let myself take pleasure in my power. Power is a balm. It heals all wounds and takes away pain, however strong it may be. It makes you lose reason.

Her dress had slipped off her right shoulder, revealing almost all of it.

Slowly, from close up, I observed the pores of her skin.

Oh, the eroticism of a woman's shoulder. Forgotten so many times and then again resurrected.

I kissed her lightly on the warm skin.

She trembled from head to toe.

Alfred walked into the room. Looking his usual sweet and slimy self. He'd recovered very well.

"Be greeted, my friend." He threw his arms open.

We didn't embrace.

I started talking in a pathetic, jerky voice.

"Alfred, you're a man of high morals. Don't object. I know you too well."

There was no sign of him objecting. He nodded smilingly.

I went into theatrical mode. Circled the room in both directions. Waved my raised right thumb high in the air. Alfred acted, too. He knew very well I knew of his pleasures. I hadn't come to him without a reason.

He was smiling widely and waiting for the cards to be put on the table.

"You're the only one I can trust with this delicate matter. It's a question of morals."

He pricked up his ears. I went on.

"I went for a walk this morning. Up into the hills, where you're nearer to God, if I may quote you."

He gave his permission by nodding.

"Just think about it. I'm walking. Threading through the thicket I come to an old, lonely, dried-up tree. An overhanging rock on the left. Another rock sticking out behind the tree."

Alfred interrupted me with a stretched out arm.

"Would you like some coffee?" he asked and looked at the girl.

I'd completely forgotten about her.

"I would," I answered.

Alfred went over to her and put his hand on her shoulder.

"Ann, dear, would you make us some coffee, please?" he asked her softly.

She ran out without looking at me.

I continued.

"What do you think I saw? A whole plantation of ganja."

Alfred wasn't smiling quite so widely anymore. He didn't know I knew of so many of his little pleasures.

"You most probably don't even know what that is. Marijuana, Alfred. Drugs."

The smile disappeared. His look became hostile.

"Immediately everything became clear to me. A whole plantation, can you imagine?"

I stopped talking and looked through the window. Sparks were still coming from the foundry chimneys.

"What happened then?" he broke the silence.

"Nothing." I turned around.

A short pause.

"You didn't report it?" A hint of fear.

"No. That's the problem. I'd never reported anybody. As you know, I'm not on the best of terms with the police."

A sigh.

"But on the other hand, a plantation like that means . . ."

I waved my arms in the air and spread them wide. In the middle of the gesture I realized I was imitating the pope.

"The owner must be a terrible drug dealer. A criminal, leading young people astray. Getting them used to poison. Killing their youth."

Nicely put.

Alfred couldn't hide his nervousness anymore.

I shook my head with exasperation and went to look at the chimneys again.

It didn't take long. He spoke again.

"And what . . . are you going to do?"

I leaped close to his face and hissed at him, "I'll report him, the bastard. Principles or no principles."

He jumped away.

"I'm going to the police this very moment. Will you come with me so that I don't change my mind on the way?"

He undid the top button on his shirt.

He was almost sure I wouldn't report him. But with a build-up like that there had to be a reason. The real matter would follow soon.

"Let him stew in his own juices for a few years and think about it. He's guilty before the law and before God. Isn't that so, Alfred?" I didn't wait for the nodding.

"Just what the pope said in his latest encyclical, am I right? They're giving young people drugs instead of poetry and culture. Oh, yes! You do some freelance work at the printers, don't you?"

Enough of the comedy. Enough jerking about. Cards on the table time. He too was visibly relieved.

"Yes," he said, "I do."

"Wouldn't they print a small book of poems for our Poet? Some five hundred copies on good quality paper. A hundred advertising posters. So that the young people get some real food instead of narcotic illusions?"

"That costs money," he mumbled.

"You're right. Why am I standing here talking about poetry? I should be at the police station."

I stepped towards the door.

We looked at each other.

We assessed each other.

"Yes, maybe it could be done," he said.

I smiled at him nicely.

"Well, you see."

We smiled at each other. When I go through the door I must be careful not to show him my back. The dirty brown of the kitchen knife handle doesn't go with the color of my jacket.

We stood there and he gave no sign of an invitation to sit down.

"What's happened to that coffee?" I asked.

He opened the door and shouted sweetly, "Annie, darling, is the coffee made?"

It was. He had to go and get it himself. The girl never appeared. I sniffed the coffee first and tried it with the tip of my tongue only. It didn't taste of bitter almonds.

We sipped from our cups.

"This is your second cup in half an hour." I pointed to the stain on the carpet. "Don't let your blood pressure rise too much."

I drained the cup right down to the dregs and put it on the bed.

"I'm going. I've got lots to do."

He didn't want to keep me there.

He went with me to the corridor.

"So it's a deal. I'll bring you all the texts and the instructions. Okay?"

"Okay," he said.

We said goodbye and I left.

The lock clicked twice behind me.

The bar was empty. I sat in my place and stared in front of me. The Cartier was almost mine. Alfred would print the book for nothing. Poet would pay me for it. I'd buy the perfume and still have quite a bit of money left. I could, of course, just ask Alfred for a bottle of Cartier as a reward for my silence. But there are gifts only women can give you.

Otherwise you have to earn them.

Boxer rolled through the door. Middle aged, stomach hanging over his trousers. He wasn't really fat, just stocky.

"Hi, Egon." He waved to me.

He didn't ask me anything. He ordered two glasses of schnapps at the bar, brought them over, put them on the table, and sat down. We shook hands.

"They've let you out then?" I started the conversation. He was taken away for alcoholism treatment every few months to a hospital, half of which was a lunatic asylum. The two parts of the hospital were separated only by some metal bars.

"Yes, they've cured me. Or so they say."

We toasted each other. He emptied his glass with that wonderful movement that only old drunks can make. The position of the bottom lip, so that it molds itself perfectly around the curve of the glass. Swallowing the liquid in the position of a sword swallower, without it touching the walls of the gullet, going straight to the stomach. Or rather straight to the pelvic bones as the stomach, liver, and kidneys have all been burnt-out by the alcohol. That's where that characteristic *splosh* originates, the one that younger and less skilled guys can't quite manage.

"The doctors still remember you," he informed me.

I nodded.

"Those from the other side," he added. Which meant those from the lunatic asylum. They probably really did still remember me. It wasn't that many years ago.

"They never wanted to tell me why they had you there."

He leaned forward and looked at me questioningly.

I smiled at him.

"I'm not gonna tell you either."

He didn't mind.

"You're right. It's none of my business. Everybody's got their own prison."

We grinned.

The schnapps had already gone from his pelvis to his prick.

"I'm going to take a piss," he said and went.

I slowly sipped the schnapps to the bottom of the glass.

He came out of the bathroom and waved to me from there.

"Hi, Egon."

He didn't ask anything. He bought two glasses of schnapps at the bar and sat down at my table.

We shook hands.

"They've let you out then?" I asked.

"Yes, they've cured me. Or so they say."

We toasted each other and drank up.

He looked at the empty glasses from the previous round and concluded, "You're doing well today."

I nodded and smiled.

The schnapps had eaten away Boxer's memory, too. Sometimes he'd think he was somewhere else, sometimes he'd think he was somebody else. He usually mixed his tenses. He was often like this. It had been known for us to say hello like this five times in succession.

He took a newspaper from his pocket and unfolded it. He put a piece of bread and three slices of salami on the table.

"Want some?"

I did. We ate up. The bread was divided in half. I got one slice of salami and he got two. He went to take a piss. He left the newspaper on the table.

This time he took a long time. I spread the paper out and glanced at the headlines. I looked at the date. It was that day's. And that was the only fresh news in these newspapers. My eyes stopped on the TV program. The clock above the bar told me I had another half an hour. Boxer came and waved to me.

"Hi, Egon."

He brought two glasses of schnapps.

"They've let you out then?" I asked.

"Yes, they've cured me. Or so they say."

We shook hands.

"Since when do you read newspapers?" he asked me and pointed to the table.

"It's today's. Do you want to read it?"

"I do."

"Just take it."

I offered him the newspaper. He took it and stuffed it in his pocket.

"Thanks," he said.

"That's all right," I nodded.

We drank up.

He pointed to the empty glasses on the table.

"You're doing well today."

I nodded.

"I don't drink as much as I used to. I'm trying to control myself. This is my first."

He put the empty glass on the table.

"But I can't take it any more. It's already gone to my head."

"I can feel it a bit, too, " I comforted him.

"I decided to have only one a day. You've got to have a strong character to keep to that. But then at least I won't have to go to that lunatic asylum. That's what's making me stick to it."

"Yes, I'm sure you won't have to go back." I got up and put my hand on his shoulder. I gave it a firm squeeze. For courage.

"I know you'll last."

"You think so?"

"I believe in you," I added firmly. "I've got to go, cheers."

"Cheers."

I set off to Karla's.

The critical hour when Karla's alarm clock usually went off was coming near. I listened in front of the door. The fuck-inducing music was already on the record player. I reached for the bell. Pulled my hand back. Hesitated. Suffered terrible torments of politeness. I rang the bell nevertheless. She wasn't expecting me. She'd put on a different face, not the one intended for me. Her features relaxed, disappeared into facelessness for a moment, and then formed themselves into the face I was used to.

"Hi, Egon."

I started, "Karla . . ."

She interrupted me. I was shooting negative answers to fast bursts of questions.

"Hungry?"

"No."

"Thirsty?"

"No."

"Horny?"

"No."

She stopped. She frowned, not understanding.

"What then?"

"Karla . . ."

"Aaaaa . . ." She realized. "Come in."

I didn't take off either my shoes or my jacket. She opened the door of a small room on the right that the architect probably designed for a nursery. Karla, at least as far as I knew, had no children. She owned a heap of old junk, mainly presents, which nearly filled the small space.

"I didn't remember straight away. You haven't been for a long time."

"Nearly a year. Will I be disturbing you?"

"No."

She took a key off the key ring and gave it to me.

"Lock behind you when you leave —"

"And put it back through the letter opening, I know."

She accompanied me to the room and turned on the light. A toilet pedestal was fixed to the middle of the ceiling. A light bulb was hidden in it, illuminating a narrow circle in the middle of the room. The heaped-up junk was lost in the semi-darkness.

She didn't step over the threshold. She was going to say something when the bell rang.

"Just go, Karla."

We looked at each other. Smiled. She went.

She closed the door behind her.

Years before she used to mix with some modernists, as they called themselves. The room was overflowing with art objects given to her as gifts. The smell of stuffiness was almost unbearable.

Directly under the light stood a huge red armchair in the shape of a five-pointed star, covered in red artificial leather. The back was shaped like a sickle, and the foot rest like a hammer. In front of the armchair stood an amateur copy of Michelangelo's *Pietà*.

Some sculpture student probably made it from plaster for practice. There was a Jesus in Mary's lap with a stomach that had been chiseled into a flat shelf, on which a portable black-and-white TV set stood. Mary was bending over across the frame towards the screen sadly. The angle stopped her from seeing anything.

I turned on the TV.

I turned the volume to the lowest audible volume. I didn't want to disturb Karla and her visitor.

I climbed into the armchair. All the remaining time before the beginning of the film I came there to see was taken up trying to get comfortable.

Without success.

I gave up with my back curled under the sickle and my legs raised high.

The fanfare sounded.

The opening screen came on:

Ingrid Bergman and Humphrey Bogart
in
CASABLANCA

The film I'd watched over and over but always in the same place. In this room. In the middle of this warehouse of abandoned and forgotten modernist junk. In this stuffiness. With Mary, reaching forward to see what it was I stared at so intently, and Jesus, who turned his head away, not because of death but because of what I could almost swear to be disgust. Opposite us hung Mona Lisa with headphones on.

When the film finished I just sat there. Not because I was particularly touched or because of the mesmerizing effect of the images. I found it hard to move because of the paralysis caused by the shape of the armchair.

I switched off the television and quietly crept through the door and across the hall. Karla's laughter could be heard from the bedroom. The man's voice was too quiet and too deep for me to be able to make out the words. I could feel it tremble in my diaphragm. Slowly, millimeter by millimeter, I unlocked the door. Closed the door and locked it again.

I closed my fist around the key, wanting to take it with me. I came as far as the middle of the corridor before changing my mind. An agreement is an agreement. I pushed it through the opening.

It clinked on the floor.

Karla's laughter changed into giggling.

It was already dark outside. I stopped and leaned on the wall in front of the entrance to the block of flats. I watched the sparks coming out of the chimneys.

I reached for the cigar but changed my mind mid-movement. Cigarettes are more suitable for short stops. I took three puffs and flicked the rest towards the starry sky. I left without waiting to see it fall.

I was overcome by two wishes incompatible with being penniless. To drink beer and to be alone. I stopped in front of the bar, peeping into the lit-up interior.

Boxer had difficulty keeping his head above the table. It swayed to and fro. Somehow I wasn't in the mood for our multiplied greetings. I could hear the clinking of full bottles. After it came the noise of raised heels.

"Hi, how are you?" Ibro shouted.

He was carting two plastic bags full of half-liter bottles of the fulfillment of my first wish.

I greeted him more pleasantly than usual.

"Where are you going?"

"I'm taking this to the dormitory. A whole week's supply."

I couldn't and I didn't want to hide my longing look.

"If you come with me we could have one or two."

I went. Took half the load. A sweet burden. I handed him the bottles through the window and then climbed in myself. The wall in the room was still divided in two. I nodded to Nastassja. I sat down on the chair next to a small cabinet separating the two beds. I took the beer out of the bag, put the lower edge of the bottle top against the wood, and hit it. I caught the foam running down the bottle with my mouth. I took a long sip. Opened another bottle for Ibro, who was sitting on his bed.

"May I ask you something?" he said timidly.

"About Ajsha?"

"Yes."

"Are you getting anywhere with her?"

"Yes. I sat opposite her at lunch."

"And?"

"She pretended not to see me."

I tried to change the subject. Convinced I wouldn't succeed.

"Where's Selim?"

"At the cinema." Ibro rolled his eyes. "He watches all the performances. Alone. He's already beaten up half the dormitory."

"Yes, I know the story. I was with him yesterday."

"I worry about him, you know." He was looking at me hesitatingly, as if not sure if I could be trusted. I helped him. "Why?"

"Well, maybe it's nothing, but . . . those photographs he put on the wall . . ."

"Yes?"

"Those are photos of naked women, aren't they?"

"Yes, of one woman, to be precise. And?"

"Yes, just that one, what's her name? Not important. At first I thought Selim put them up like any other man does. To help him jerk himself off. So that he doesn't have to go through the cupboard if he needs them in a hurry. You understand?"

"I understand." I had difficulties hiding my smile.

"I'll give you an example. I'm lying on the bed reading comics, when Selim gets up from his bed, stands in front of the photos, and stares at them. I think, he'll do it now, so I go out to the corridor not to disturb him. I come back after ten minutes or half an hour and he's still standing motionless just like he was when I went."

"You mean he's not jerking himself off?"

"Yes, and that's what's worrying me. It isn't normal. Is he sick or something?"

I nodded.

"You're right. There is something wrong there."

Ibro decided to tell me everything.

"Egon, don't take this personally but . . . how shall I put this . . . you two are somehow similar —"

I interrupted him.

"You mean I don't jerk myself off either?"

"Don't be like that, that's not what I meant . . . I'm sure you do . . ."

"How do you know that?"

"Well . . . I don't really . . . I . . ."

He got confused and waved his arms. The breeze they made couldn't blow away the redness on his cheeks.

I savored his embarrassment for another second and then stopped his torment.

"It's all right. I do understand what you're trying to say. Just relax."

The last sentence was intended for his toes, which were waiting in readiness by the edge of his shoes, slipping in slowly.

He did as told and took off his winkle-pickers.

A terrible stench.

"Are you angry?" he asked.

"No. Why?"

He was watching me with fear, as if expecting me to bite him any minute. I took a sip from the bottle.

"Just wondered. . . . Maybe you're not comfortable talking about this."

"No less than talking about anything else."

Ibro stood the empty bottle by the bed. He opened another one.

I followed his example.

"Egon," he started, "you don't mind if I lie down, I'm so tired."

I shrugged my shoulders.

Ibro sprawled on the bed. Bent the pillow over to raise his head, holding the bottle on his stomach between his hands.

"The work tires me out," he apologized once more.

"It's all right."

I switched on the lamp on the cabinet and turned off the light.

We emptied the bottles. Third round.

He broke the silence.

"What do you think of Ajsha?"

A sudden attack of honesty even though it was of no interest to me. It wasn't my problem.

"I don't know if you're the right one for her."

"You think so?"

"You'd better give up."

Silence fell.

We spoke again during the fourth round.

First he gave a sigh, long and sad.

"You're probably right, but I can't help it. I've fallen in love."

"That's true, too."

"She's my first love."

First loves hurt most. I felt sorry for him.

"There was another woman. A middle-aged widow. I thought I loved her, but that was nothing compared to this."

Ibro stared at the ceiling and talked, clutching the bottle. He wasn't drinking anymore. I opened another one for myself only.

"She always smiled at me when she went to work in the fields."

He stopped talking. I took the cigar out of my pocket and lit it. This was the right moment. I had plenty of time. Ibro was at that stage of talking when he didn't need a listener anymore. But it's still nice to have somebody there so that you don't talk to the walls.

He sighed again. I was watching the smoke curling in the light from the lamp.

"I'm still a virgin," he said.

I didn't say anything.

"Ajsha must need somebody with experience. What can she do with me? I don't know how to approach her. What to say, what to do."

I looked for an ashtray and remembered that both he and Selim were non-smokers. I shook the cigar into the empty bottle and managed to get half the ash on the floor. Ibro talked without a break. I pulled the Rimbaud out of my pocket, read a few poems, and put the book back again. I opened another beer.

"I was grazing sheep at granddad Mehmet's one day. . . ."

My tongue started burning. I wasn't trying to get the ash in the bottle anymore. I just shook the cigar over the floor.

"I liked it really. After that I did it every day."

Another beer. I stared in front of me. If I moved my head quickly the room lost definition. The view multiplied.

"Once my granddad caught me. I nearly died with embarrassment. . . ."

I bent forward. Put my elbows on my knees. Smoked the cigar. Belched. Ibro wasn't disturbed.

"Everybody found out, the whole village. Granddad told them."

I'd smoked two thirds of the cigar already. Blue smoke was floating around the room.

"And that widow laughed at me. She shouted after me whenever we met. Little boy! Do you still let the sheep lick your willy? That's exactly what she used to shout. I was dying with embarrassment. . . ."

The factory siren went off. Slowly, risking the failure of my sight, I turned my head towards the window. It was night outside. All I could see was the reflection of the room in the window. A guy lying on the bed, talking in a monotonous voice, just about to fall asleep, and another guy sitting on a chair next to the top of the bed, bent forward, leaning his chin on his palm. A fortnight's stubble. A cigar in his mouth. I started shaking. I went to the window and opened it. I was convinced that I would see the streets of Vienna from the turn of the century. Coaches on the roads. I was looking at the foundry but couldn't recognize it. I ran my hand over my forehead, wondering where and who I was. When I was. Were my visions returning? Was I *floating* again, into the worlds of stories I'd heard, or read, or written? I was losing myself. If I didn't hold on, I'd be lost. Again, like all those times before. The doctors called it *issues of identity. Loss of the self.* I had to hold on. I threw the cigar down and vomited over the windowsill. There was nobody on the road. The sound of a crane moving helped me to catch the space and time. I looked at Ibro asleep on the bed.

I closed the window and stepped into the corridor. Most of my strength was taken up by trying to control my legs. I had to take a shit. I stepped inside the bathroom and nearly drowned in the sea of sewage on the floor. Balancing on the tips of my toes, I made my way to the toilet. There was no toilet paper, of course. I went back to the sleeping Ibro, fumbled through the cupboard, and went back with a packet of toilet paper. I splashed back to the shitting position.

It was difficult. Bloody difficult.

Standing on the tips of my toes, I pulled my trousers and my underpants down to my knees, sacrificed the right hand for holding them there, while lifting my jacket up with my left hand so as not to shit on it. I was clutching the paper between my lips. I pushed my ass back. My head was nearly on my knees. I was just about to start. With my right hand I just managed to catch the Rimbaud, which slid out of my pocket. I saved my trousers from falling into the flood by quickly spreading my knees. I pushed the book back into my pocket and grabbed hold of my trousers. I leaned forward and again only just caught the poem collection. I nearly lost my balance and fell into the stinking mess on the floor. The water had already gone below deck and wet my socks. At last I realized why all the inhabitants of the dormitory wore shoes with raised heels.

My bowels were letting me know they wouldn't stand for this messing around, delaying things much longer. I wanted to stick Rimbaud in my mouth, but was afraid to open it and lose the paper. I was beginning to panic.

"Think," I said to myself. Quietly, of course, because of the full mouth.

And I thought. I pulled my trousers up again and waded to the corridor and put Rimbaud on the radiator. I turned the front of the book up so that REMBO could be seen. So that nobody would think it was a pulp with the adventures of Wyatt Earp. I ran back to the toilet and took my shit.

There was no soap. Only cold water came out of the tap. I rubbed my hands and shook the drops off my fingers and stepped out, leaving wet footprints behind me. On the way to the exit window, I reached for the book. It wasn't there.

With both hands I felt the whole of the top of the radiator ribs, looked behind the radiator and under it, I even knelt down to see better.

Finally I grasped the indisputable fact. The Rimbaud wasn't there anymore.

It had disappeared.

I searched all around the radiator. Ran up and down the corridor looking for the book. It wasn't there.

You adjust your expectations to the world around you. Everything around you depends on constants that are so ordinary and unchangeable that you pay no attention to them. It took some time before I dared say it out loud and even longer to grasp it:

IN THE MIDDLE OF THE DORMITORY SOMEBODY HAD NICKED RIMBAUD'S POETRY.

The world had collapsed. As if a stone dropped from a hand had hung in the air. It was unimaginable. I was struck by terror. Panic. All drunkenness disappeared in a moment. My brains were rattling in a hellish rhythm.

There was no logical explanation. None.

I knew most of the inhabitants. There wasn't one poetry lover among them. Those who would take a book like that have never even ventured into a dormitory. I thought about the cleaner. I ran to the end of the corridor and looked around. The bin was full of garbage and paper, but no book.

Maybe somebody took it to put it under a rickety table or wardrobe. The probability of that was very small.

I was in the bathroom for three, maybe four minutes. And just then somebody needing a book of that thickness would walk past.

My brain was trying to patch up the logical world, which had fallen apart.

It you remove a little stone, the whole sphere around you collapses.

Suddenly I became aware of a terrible smell, which I smelled every day. I should've been used to it completely but it still hit me with all its strength and clarity.

It stank of sulfur.

At the same time as the smell hit me, a sentence from Spränger's book, the one about there not being anything inexplicable in this world. Those things that seem inexplicable fall into the sphere of demonology.

Footsteps could be heard in the corridor. I pressed myself against the radiator, trembling with fear. The footsteps were coming nearer. The hard sounds of hooves. With my back against the wall, I slid into a squat.

From around the corner came a thin guy with huge winkle-pickers. He noticed me and immediately looked down. He was probably more scared than I had been earlier. He sped up, staring in front of him, and disappeared up the stairs.

The presence of another human being helped me. The world was still holding together. Maybe I'll manage to put my missing stone back in. A lot of things that seem inexplicable at a certain moment are explained later on.

I decided to wait. I had no other option. I jumped onto the road and set off home. The wind was taking the clouds of smoke from the tops of the chimneys and blowing them towards me.

I pushed my hand under my jacket and felt the T-shirt on my back. It was soaking wet. I trembled in the cold.

I couldn't get rid of the feeling that something was sitting on my neck.

The whole way home I tried to stop my body from running. A headless rush.

It clouded over. The sky was completely black without a ribbon of light. The air was heavy and thick with smoke, which was settling on the ground and dissolving the outlines of the blocks of flats under the weak light of the streetlights. A dead cat lay on the ground, its innards squeezed out onto the road.

The smell of sulfur was getting stronger and stronger.

PART TWO

Hell is more bearable than nothingness.
— *P.J. Bailey, "Festus"*

CHAPTER 6

For two weeks, I didn't see any of the people I talked about earlier. I wasn't there. I was absent, as they say at school. After I got back, the first thing I did was to take a walk along the foundry. With my ears and eyes open. Looking for any changes. There weren't any. There never are.

A note was stuck in my door. It told me to collect the books. Alfred's signature, dated the day before. I took a shower and set off to see Poet. I didn't have to climb the fence. Marble stairs, guarded by a female guard, led to his place. Before she let me go up the stairs she made a phone call.

Poet's office was on the first floor.

He had his head stuck between two heaps of paper.

"The books are printed."

His face lit up.

"Did you bring a copy?"

"No," I shook my head, thinking of how I could politely remind him of the payment.

There was no need to do anything.

"If you meet me when I finish work, we'll go to the bank together to get the money."

"Okay." I waved Alfred's note in front of him. "This is a receipt with which you can get the books."

I put it in my pocket.

He opened a drawer in his desk and pulled out a bottle of red wine.

We toasted each other. To success. That was his suggestion, not mine.

He looked at his watch.

"Half past ten. Another three and a half hours."

I left him stewing with impatience and counting the minutes.

I went to the bar. I saw Karla through a supermarket window. She was just paying.

She grinned at me from ear to ear, all the way to the door, carrying two full grocery bags.

"Hi, Egon."

"Hi," I said hesitantly. I found her cheerfulness suspicious. I wasn't used to it.

She put the bags on the floor. From the top of one of them she produced a booklet, printed on the worst possible paper.

"Look."

I took it. It was the romance I'd written. It had been published very quickly. I couldn't see anything unusual about it, no reason for Karla to be so amused. The cover was in the usual style. Two lovers on the spring grass. They had left my title. *Naked and Barefoot*, it said.

"I don't understand, what's this got to do with me?"

I gave the book back to Karla.

She grinned even wider and pushed the cover right in front of my eyes. I looked at the photo. Read the writing twice before it dawned on me.

"Ooooooh, shit," I said with great difficulty.

I knew the editor wouldn't forgive me my outbursts in his office. He'd published the novel under my real name. No English female name. Egon Surname was what was under the title.

Karla became serious.

"You're blushing, you know?"

I didn't know whether to believe her or not. I couldn't feel a gush of blood in my cheeks.

"Now you can start apologizing."

"I'll just explain."

"It's the same thing."

"Yes, I suppose."

"Let's go to the bar. I don't want to listen to stories in the middle of the street."

She ordered coffee with cream and a beer. She opened the packet and poured the sugar into the hole she'd made with a teaspoon in the whipped cream.

"As a matter of fact, I'd often wondered what you did for a living."

I told her I'd had a fight with the editor and that this was his revenge. I told her his real name. She started laughing. She laughed even more when I told her some other names hiding under English pseudonyms.

She asked me if I knew the person writing under a French-sounding name.

"I don't know all of them. I only found out about the ones I told you by chance."

"It's me," she said.

We looked at each other. Felt laughter growing inside us. It exploded. We roared with laughter, nudging each other with our elbows. I looked around.

The surprised, already accusing looks of the waitress and the pensioners made me laugh even louder.

She told me a few names of the writers of love stories she knew. There was no end to our amusement.

"Karla, you're the only woman who can still surprise me after all these years."

She became serious, sipped her coffee, and added, "You, too, sometimes."

"You didn't know?"

"I didn't. Even though you're the right sort of person for these things."

I frowned and looked at her angrily, with exaggeration and not really meaning it.

"Thanks."

"Nothing to thank me for."

"No, there isn't."

I poured the beer and emptied my glass.

"I call this penetration into the very essence of stupidity. Give me the book. I've got to look at something."

I took the book, turned a few pages, and found the sentence I was looking for.

"They didn't leave it out. Listen to the latest result of my searching."

I cleared my throat. Waited a moment. Then read, "She sighed as if she'd been stabbed by a penis. Oh!"

Laughter again.

"I'm surprised they left it in. Usually they don't leave in any words that might offend the puritans."

"It's supposed to be an illustration of how low an author can fall when published under his real name."

She looked at her watch. I knew what she was going to say.

"I'm late. I've got to go. Bye."

I puckered my lips.

"A kiss?"

She looked at me as if she was hesitating. And then nodded.

"Aren't you afraid that some fine gentleman in his prime might see you?"

She immediately reciprocated.

"Aren't you afraid that some girl at the sweetest time of her life might see you?"

"Let's do it secretly."

"And quickly."

We looked around to see if anybody was looking at us.

Everybody was.

We kissed.

"Let's go," she said.

I helped her carry her bags. She unlocked her door and turned around.

"I really am in a hurry."

But there was still time for a long kiss. That's what the Hollywood movies had taught us. In a house on fire, on a sinking ship, or in any other impossible situation thought up by a script writer, there's always time for a kiss.

I went to the bar to wait for Poet to finish work. Hippy sat alone at a table in an empty bar. I hadn't even sat down properly when he started to express his shock. I knew a lot of people read trashy novels but I never thought everybody did. I don't read them. Honestly. I just write the odd one.

I didn't make the effort to explain why it had been published under my real name. I did tell him the names of the editor and a few other authors, though.

He laughed from the bottom of his heart.

At that moment I realized the power of the media. The editor printed my name. At least half a million people knew it now. I repeated the editor's name twice and was already fed up with saying it. At the thought of having to repeat it another four hundred and ninety-nine thousand nine hundred and ninety-eight times in order to get even, I decided to give up.

"I understand, you need the money," started Hippy, "but still, it's crap what you write. You should take a pen and use your talent, if you have any, to improve the world."

I leaned forward and started talking with a voice used for telling deep secrets, when you want lots of people to find out about them.

"Listen, Hippy," I looked him in the eyes, "do you really believe?"

"In what?"

"That it's possible to change the world with writing?"

"I do."

"There you go then. Me, too. That's precisely why I'm writing cheap paperbacks. On top of the financial reasons, of course."

He looked at me idiotically. He didn't understand anything anymore.

"I'll explain. If I wrote moralistic tragedies, they'd say I was just another preacher. If I was writing any kind of literature that you call art, only a handful of people would read me. A closed circle. Other writers reading the works of their colleagues. Outside that small group of people, nobody gives a shit about those works. That's how it really is."

He thought for a bit before he nodded.

"Look, I write a romantic novel. More erotic than romantic. Let's call it what it really is: a fuck novel. People read it. Many people. They get excited. They become lustful. They need a fuck. They'd like to re-enact one or two scenes from the book. They go and try it out. They fuck. Can you imagine? A large number of excited readers rolling on beds. And what are you like after a good fuck? Tired and satisfied. A crowd of tired and satisfied readers. A lot of energy going into fucking. Immense quantities. Energy that would otherwise have been used for fighting and being nasty to each other. And look, the world has changed a little bit. For the better. There you are."

He was looking at me with his eyes wide open. He couldn't believe it.

"I'd never expect you to make a speech like that."

"I do occasionally surprise people."

"You certainly do."

The justification of the fuck novels from the nirvanistic standpoint made me terribly thirsty. I looked around. At that moment Sheriff came in. I said goodbye to Hippy and sat at a different table. I pulled out a chair for Sheriff. He sat next to me and ordered two beers.

He was already in his civilian clothes. So he must have escaped from the foundry before the end of his shift. He was about my age. A leader of quite a large circle of western lovers. They wore cowboy outfits, or what they thought cowboys wore. Sheriff outdid them all. All the others wore ordinary hats; he was the only one wearing a real Stetson. A white one, like Tom Mix. A denim suit and a red scarf around his neck. They all wore boots. Black or brown pointed things with raised heels. His were made of snake skin. With silver spurs.

He must have spent a fortune on them. He had his sources, which he used to obtain the clothes he wanted. He never told anybody who his connections were. The novices had to find their own way. He had a crew cut. He was smoothly shaven with a real razor, not just a razor blade. His neck was shaven, too. He hated blacks. I doubt he'd ever seen one. The worse insult he would utter before a fight was to call somebody a Yankee. I'd visited him at the dormitory. He'd hung an enormous Confederate flag on the wall. A poster on each side of the door. On one there was Clint Eastwood, tied up, naked down to his waist and with pistols in his hands. On the other was Clint in a poncho, sitting on a horse, unshaven, with a cigar butt in his mouth.

When he'd get drunk, which only happened occasionally, he'd wish he'd been born in Texas and not here.

Had he really been born in Texas and that was the only change in the story of his life, he'd have been born black.

I'd never said that to him or teased him with it. Just the fact that he claimed I was the only one he trusted with his secret wishes and troubles was useful to me sometimes. For a beer, paid for by him, or for saving me from a circle of guys eager to fight because I'd offended them. And not last because I was probably the only man in town who was allowed to call his beloved Clint by a nickname in his presence.

"I've got something for you," he said. "Is this yours?"

He pulled a small book out of his pocket and put it on the table. I couldn't believe it. My bottom jaw dropped.

It was the Rimbaud. The very same one that got lost, disappeared, went missing at the dormitory.

"Hey, where did you get it?"

"My roommate threw it in the bin. After cursing like a Yankee. He'd made a mistake. He'd walked down the corridor and saw the book on the radiator. He thought it was a comic. He looked at the title to see if he'd already read it. It said REMBO. And he thought to himself, 'Oh, look, so they started publishing the adventures of Sylvester Stallone here, too.' He took it and noticed his mistake when he got to the room. He threw it away. I looked to see what'd made him so angry and thought it must be yours. Had you forgotten it there?"

"Yes, I'd forgotten it."

"Okay."

"Thanks."

"It's all right. I'd been carrying it with me for two weeks, but you were nowhere to be seen."

We toasted to General Lee and drank up our beers.

"Sheriff, I'd like to ask you a small favor."

"Yeah?"

"Could you bring your cowboys to the bookstore tonight at six?"

"Why?"

"Poet'll be reading his poems."

"And you're the organizer?"

"I am, I admit it. And how successful it'll be depends on you."

He emptied his glass and nodded.

"All right, we'll come. How long will it last?"

"Half an hour, no more."

"Okay."

The foundry sirens went off. Time to meet Poet.

I got up and nodded to Sheriff.

"Say hello to Scarlett. Cheers."

He grinned and spat between his teeth.

"Yankee," I heard behind my back.

I went out. Crowds were pouring out of the foundry and the secondary school. I was looking out for Long Legs. It wasn't difficult to spot her.

She was a lot taller than her schoolmates. When she went past we looked at each other. I joined the crowd with my eyes glued to her hair. I zigzagged among the workers, bumping into school bags, saying hello to acquaintances, slowly approaching her. I bumped into somebody. I jumped to the left, not wanting to take my eyes off Long Legs for fear of losing sight of her, launched forward and again the same body got in my way.

"I'm here. It's me you're looking for, isn't it?" said Poet.

Long Legs disappeared in the crowd. I wanted to tell him to wait a bit, but he already had both his hands on my collar.

"Let's go get the books, let's go get the books," like a stuck record.

And we went.

They weren't very glad to see us at the printers. They were just about to leave. Alfred was firmly formal. Sign here, sign there. Poet looked as if he was giving his autograph. With great pleasure. We all shook hands and we found ourselves on the doorstep with the packets of books. Poet went to borrow a car from somebody while I sat on the books, smoking. I tore the wrapping and looked at a copy. A thin but neat book. Poet had brought me a whole parcel of poems. I gave half to Alfred for printing and he then printed half of those. It really was Selected Works. There was a folder with posters, too.

Poet returned with the car. We loaded the packets. He looked through the book and was visibly satisfied. We drove to the bank, where I waited in the car until he came back with the money. I felt the envelope and stashed it in my pocket. I didn't count the money.

I told him that he had a reading organized for six o'clock that evening at the bookstore. He started panicking. He had to rush home to have a wash, iron his suit, have a shave, etcetera.

He complained that nobody would turn up as there were no ads for it.

"Were you listening to the local radio station yesterday at four?"

"No."

"They announced your reading."

And I added that he still had enough time to call everybody and tell them about it. He drove off.

On my way home I stopped at the bookstore. I told the assistant about the book promotion and so on. She went to tell her boss. I convinced her as well. But we were only given one corner at the back for no longer than half an hour.

I left a couple of posters with her. For sticking in the window. I stuck three on notice boards on the way home.

I counted the money at the flat. He hadn't cheated me.

I opened the Bible and put the notes between the pages, one at a time. I got as far as Exodus. My biggest financial success so far.

I stashed a few notes in my pockets, just in case, and went out.

Ajsha was walking on the opposite side of the road. I waved to her, she smiled, and I ran across the road. She was looking at me as if I had put on gold plating in the time since she'd last seen me.

"I didn't know you were a writer," she said.

"Well . . . well . . ." I dithered.

She couldn't take her eyes off me.

"I've never met a writer before."

I was beginning to like it. The editor's revenge did have some good sides.

"Well, you know how it is . . . we writers . . . blablablabla . . ."

"Oh, really?"

"Yeah, blablablablablabla . . ."

"Oh," she could only sigh.

I invited her for a drink.

She came.

She ordered a Coca-Cola, I ordered a beer.

I looked around to make sure nobody I knew was within earshot and then opened all the valves.

"Blablablablablablablablablablabla . . ."

It bowled her over, she was barely conscious anymore.

I don't usually do such stupid things, but when I do lose the ground under my feet I hang high up in the air. She wasn't a quiet sort, and yet she could only get a word in edgeways when my mouth was full of beer. She was on her way to the dentist and she was already late. She showed me the tooth that needed filling. I looked in her mouth. Very exciting tonsils.

She went. I ordered another beer.

I'd only just started drinking when Ibro sat down next to me.

"What did she say?" he asked even before his seat got warm.

"Are you following her?"

"Well . . . just sometimes . . . a little," he admitted between blushing and playing with his feet.

"She's going to the dentist."

He went over the gaps in his mouth with his fingers and sighed.

"I should go, too. Where do you register?"

"You'll find out next time you follow her."

"Egon, can I ask you something?"

"No," I said.

He collapsed with sadness.

He shut up and looked at the table in front of him.

"What is it?"

"There's a dance tomorrow. Would you invite Ajsha for me?"

"No, Ibro," I shook my head, "you invite your women yourself."

He became sad again.

I thought that maybe I was being too hard on him.

"Maybe, I'll see. I'm not promising anything. Okay?"

His whole face was smiling. He ordered two beers. We toasted each other.

"Brilliant, you're a real pal. Seriously."

"Ibro, listen. I didn't promise anything. Anything."

He nodded, still smiling. He winked at me with an I-know-you look in his eyes. His familiarity started to annoy me. I didn't say anything anymore. Any future disappointments would be his own doing.

"Today is a good day. All good news."

"What news?"

"I got my first check today. Tomorrow I've got a day off. I'm going to Italy to buy a new suit and shoes. In the evening Ajsha will come to the dance, and I'll be there in all my new gear. And tonight my three brothers are coming to visit."

"Are they going to work at the foundry?"

"No, no," he shook his head as if he'd heard the most stupid thing in the world.

"They're working in Germany. They'd been at home for a week and now they're visiting me on the way back."

My brains rattled with calculations.

"They're going to Germany, you say?"

"Yes." He looked at me questioningly.

"Do you think they could bring something for me?"

He hesitated.

"A television set? Something big?"

I laughed with relief.

"No, something very small. A bottle of perfume."

"The one you used to wear?"

"Yes."

"No problem."

"Really?"

"Certainly. You write down what you want and you'll get it.

Or even better. Be at the station around nine tonight, before the train for Munich leaves."

"I'll be there."

"It's a deal."

"But you'll still ask them before if they're willing to do me a favor."

"Okay, I'll ask them, but I'm telling you, they'll bring it definitely. A favor for a favor. Isn't that so? That's what friends are for."

I remembered my conditional agreement to invite Ajsha to the dance. Maybe I really would. If I bumped into her accidentally. I wouldn't go looking for her.

"What if she doesn't want to come?"

"She'll come, definitely. You just ask her."

"I will."

I could always tell him that she didn't want to come. Before he plucked up enough courage to go and ask her if that was true, we'd all be old age pensioners.

"Tonight, straight after my brothers have left, I must go to bed. I have to be well rested for tomorrow. But Selim bothers me. He doesn't say anything but he still bothers me. I just can't get used to it. I wake up in the middle of the night and I watch him."

He sighed deeply. As if he'd buried all his hopes.

"What's the matter with Selim?"

"What? You don't know?" Ibro was surprised. He couldn't believe that I hadn't heard the news yet.

"I don't know, I haven't been around for a while."

"True, I haven't seen you. He's standing. . . ."

"What do you mean, he's standing?"

"He's standing on one leg."

"Why, what for, how, tell me!"

"He's been standing on one leg in the middle of the room for three days and three nights, not saying anything. He eats what I bring him, but he doesn't put his other foot down. I wake in the night to see if he's gone to sleep. And he is asleep. On one leg. He wants to be mentioned in some book or something."

I understood.

I quickly finished my beer.

"Let's go."

"Are you going to talk to him?"

"Yes."

"I was going to ask you to do that. Only you can persuade him to stop."

Ibro paid for all the drinks. We half ran to the dormitory. Selim, for fuck's sake, when is your madness going to end? I'd always assumed he'd calm down, that he wouldn't fall into the black hole of his obsession. But I knew that he had an explosive nature, and that I had a certain influence on him. I felt partly responsible.

"Talk him into giving up," Ibro said on the way. "You know, when I bring Ajsha to the room tomorrow after the dance, and like, Selim is standing in the middle of the room, not moving, not saying anything. . . . You know what I mean? Otherwise I could ask him to stay at a friend's overnight."

I looked at him angrily. He shut up and didn't say a word the rest of the way.

I climbed through the window and waited for Ibro in front of the door to their room.

"You stay here. I'll talk to him on my own."

"Okay."

I knocked and went in.

Selim stood on one leg facing the window. Looking at the foundry chimneys.

He didn't turn to look at me.

I stood in front of him, blocking his view.

Not a twitch. He was looking through me. If he could see anything anymore.

"Hello, Selim."

He didn't answer. Nothing changed on his face.

I lit a cigarette.

"You want to get into the *Guinness Book of World Records*, eh?"

I may as well have been talking to the wall.

"You found a way of becoming well known. An equal to Nastassja. Before you go to Rome, if she's still there, and stand before her. . . ."

He didn't say either yes or no. I went on.

"Think about it Selim. I'm relying on you having some brains left. You usually use them. Have you ever seen that book?"

He remained motionless.

I continued with the voice of an old lady telling her cat not to shit on the Persian carpet.

"Quite a large book. At least three hundred pages. A new edition every year. And thousands of mugs like you in it. Twenty per page. At the very least. In small print. You'll still only be one of many. She won't even hear about you."

The cat went on shitting wherever it felt like.

"It means nothing, fame acquired with these records. Saccharin for those who can't get real sugar. And something else. Listen carefully. To accept your achievement for publication in the next edition, I seem to think you have to have at least two witnesses who are present at all times and you have to notify the publishers beforehand of the exact date of the beginning of your endeavor. Maybe they even send somebody to witness it. And what did you do? You stood in the middle of a room like a stork and hey, bingo, there's your record. Who's gonna believe you? Ibro is at work in the morning. You could be lying on the bed in the meantime. In the afternoons he's out, at night he sleeps. It could be that you were only standing there when somebody was looking at you. I do believe you. But nobody else will."

My voice was becoming pleading, and there was a hint of desperation in it.

Suddenly I felt like crying, "There's no point, Selim! Everything's useless!"

He was still staring through me.

My desperation turned to rage.

"Listen to me carefully." I leaned forward, face to face, eyes to eyes. "I'll go out now. I'll smoke a cigarette in front of the door. Think about it. If you've got any sense left you'll come out. I'll come back and ask you what you think. If you decide to continue with this, we'll pack you up and send you to Madame Tussauds. We'll leave you alone then. So, it's up to you."

I left the room and Ibro pounced on me immediately.

"What happened, did you succeed?"

"He's thinking, let's wait five minutes."

I lit a cigarette and smoked it slowly, dragging it out. I rolled every puff around my mouth three times. I was convinced he'd come. The door stayed closed. I put the cigarette out. I gave him another two minutes. He didn't come. I looked in. He was still standing like before.

I closed the door in Ibro's face and stepped in front of Selim.

Two streams of tears were running down his cheeks.

"What's the matter, aren't you going to stand on both feet?"

Finally he spoke. He said, "I would, but I can't."

He sobbed.

I went out and told Ibro that Selim had given in. Told him to call an ambulance and a doctor. They'd get him back on both feet. If his left leg hadn't dried up completely.

Ibro ran into the room, came back and went to make a call from the porter's office.

I jumped through the window and went to the bar.

I washed away the time with beer before Poet's presentation.

I got to the bookstore early. Besides me and the star of the evening there was the circle of culture lovers. Both aging groupies included. The poisonous one looked at me slightly more kindly, or maybe it just seemed so to me. At five minutes before six, Poet went to stand in the middle of the circle of chairs. He was holding his book in his hands, looking at me with desperation. My eyes kept glancing at the clock on the wall and I got nervous, too.

Exactly at six, the left and right half of the door opened with a loud bang. Sheriff entered. With his belt hanging low. Behind him one by one came his cowboys. The bookstore suddenly seemed like the OK Corral. They sat down.

The literary evening started ten minutes late because of the performer's astonishment.

Sheriff took off his Stetson and put it on his knees. The other hats followed as one.

Poet started reading. At first he could hardly get the words out, but slowly he got into it, and by the end he was really lively. He stopped. I clapped. The cowboys stamped their boots and threw their hats in the air. I winked to Sheriff, congratulated Poet, and left. It was a nice literary evening. One of the best I'd ever attended.

Back at the flat, I had a shower and took a bunch of bank notes out of the Bible.

I went to a restaurant and treated myself to a meal.

Just before nine, I got to the railway station. Ibro was already saying goodbye to his brothers.

They were smaller than him. Stocky, like wrestlers. All three dressed in identical suits, black with narrow stripes. They were so alike they looked like triplets. Next to them, Ibro looked as if he hadn't been quite finished.

We shook hands.

Ibro introduced us.

"This is my friend, who's asked me to ask you to bring him something."

They nodded.

"Something small. Perfume. The name is on this paper."

I gave the paper to the middle one. He read it out loud. Letter by letter, exactly as it was written.

"Cartier pour l'homme."

"How much does it cost?" asked the one on the left.

I told him and gave him the money. They looked at each other.

"Is it for a woman?"

"Yes," I said with embarrassment, "women have to be spoiled."

Ibro rolled his eyes.

"They have to be beaten," the middle one firmly corrected me and took the money. "All right, it's a deal. We won't be coming until the summer but there are plenty of our friends who go home every week. We'll give the perfume to one of them. He'll give it to our brother. It could be here in a couple of days."

That made me happy.

"Great."

"Does that suit you?"

"Yeah."

"It won't be too late, it's not her birthday or something?" asked the one on the left.

"Yes, but not until next week."

Ibro afforded himself another circle with his eyes.

"You'll definitely get it by then," nodded the middle one.

We shook hands.

"We've got to get on the train."

They walked in my direction. I walked with Ibro along the long train.

Their compartment was in the next to last carriage. The end of the train was in the middle of the bridge over the road. We stopped and looked at the cars below us.

"Another piss, and then we're off to Germany," said one of the brothers and stood next to the fence. The other two followed.

They stood next to each other pissing on the cars driving past under the bridge.

Ibro and I walked on slowly. We stopped at their carriage and I lit up. A policeman came by, looked at us, and then noticed the brothers pissing.

"Hey!!! What are you doing? Stop!!!" he shouted. He ran past us to the brothers and started shouting at them. They didn't even look at him.

He went mad with fury. He was young, probably a beginner, the same height as them, but slighter.

They shook their willies, put them back in their trousers, and then slowly turned around. The cop was roaring like the MGM lion.

Suddenly, as if they'd trained for it, the brothers started beating him with their fists. The cop couldn't even fall. The blows from all directions held him upright. When he started looking like an empty sack, they grabbed him, one by his collar, one by the trousers on his ass, and the third one by his legs, and took him to a dumpster standing in the bushes ten meters away. They threw him in. One of them came back for his hat, which was lying on the ground, picked it up and threw it in the garbage, too, and closed the lid.

We shook hands again. They noticed my surprise. It bordered on enthusiasm.

"What's the matter, don't you treat them like this here?" the middle one asked.

"No, definitely not."

"It's a custom where we come from."

"In Germany?"

They looked at me as if I was an idiot.

"No. Germany is something else. At home. The police, ticket collectors, gas and electricity meter readers, and so on. . . ."

"A nice custom," I had to admit. "It might be worth introducing it here."

The brothers embraced and kissed and jumped on the train, which was already moving. Ibro and I waved.

"What brothers I have! Did you see that?" he turned to me enthusiastically. I had to admit they were admirable.

"How's Selim?"

"I don't know. They took him away in an ambulance. He had to lie on his stomach on the stretcher, because of his leg, you know."

We said goodbye.

Ibro set off for the dormitory, and I went in the opposite direction. I felt like sleeping even though it was still early.

On the way, I remembered the policeman's look. He had seen me, and he must have remembered me. He knows where to find me. It's going to be a difficult day tomorrow.

A painful day.

The lights by the rail track turned to red.

In the block of flats I was walking past, somebody turned off the radio.

CHAPTER 7

I got up early, had a shower, got dressed, and sat down. I didn't have to wait at all, they came immediately. Banging on the door. I'd already unlocked it. Two of them fell in, grabbed me, and shoved me down the corridor. A Black Maria was waiting outside. Maybe they thought they'd manage to get all five of us in one go. That I'd immediately give them the addresses of my friends. I didn't. And they didn't ask me for them anyway.

I sat in the part of the van with mesh on the windows, surprised at how short the journey was. It could've done with being longer. They took me to an office and pushed me onto a chair. Opposite me sat an old policeman with glasses, scribbling on some paper. I had to give him my personal details.

He didn't ask for my rank and number.

I was passed onto somebody else. Somebody young. He took me to wait in a room with bars on the windows. In the doorway he hit me twice in the kidneys. On the left and the right side. It helped. After a long time without it, I was reminded of the feeling of physical pain. They didn't take my cigarettes away. I smoked three. One after the other.

A third policeman came to take me to a room similar to

the one I was in before. An empty room. This one gave me a slightly friendlier shove towards the wall before he left. Five more cigarettes. My stomach was like a hard ball. It twitched occasionally. I needed a piss. I thought about pissing through the bars when a new face came for me. Soon I'd see the whole place. This one could speak. He didn't shove me to the next room. "Comrade, come with me!" he said.

And then I knew I was in deep shit. If somebody calls you "comrade" in this country, either he is afraid of you or you should be afraid of him.

I'd already seen the ground floor. I was expecting the basement, but he took me to the second floor instead. I'd never been there before. I started getting worried.

He knocked on a door without a name on it and waited for somebody to answer before he opened it. He was respectful and humble. I went in. The policeman left me alone with an older man behind a desk. He wasn't busy with papers. He was sitting there looking at me. He invited me to sit down. He offered me a cigarette. We lit up. As far as I could see, he wasn't in a uniform. A pair of civilian trousers and a police shirt, or at least one with a similar cut, with epaulettes, no rank. His movements expressed power and authority, but not in a theatrical, showy sort of way. Very polite and civilized. An image of a good father. Had he been stupid, he'd have started the conversation with "let's be friends." But he wasn't stupid.

Anything but. He was dangerous, I could feel that even though there was no confirmation of that feeling in his behavior. He must have been over fifty. It was hard to judge his age because he had the dried-up and wrinkled face of a heavy smoker.

"I'm not from this town," he said. "I'm here on a business visit, let's say. Our talk isn't obligatory and it's not a questioning. I happened to hear that they'd brought you in. Another cigarette?"

I was just putting one out into an overflowing ashtray. I accepted the offer and we lit up again.

He went on.

"Well then, what do we know? Or rather, what do the police here know? Three unidentified men yesterday beat up a cadet and threw him in a dumpster. He described you, but he didn't recognize any of the others. He'll be in the hospital for at least three weeks and off work for at least three more. On top of that there's an old age pensioner who's in the hospital, too, from shock brought on by finding him when getting rid of her trash. She's got heart disease, and excitement of that kind could be very harmful to her."

I was biting my lips to stop myself from laughing. Somehow I succeeded.

"We know — that is, they know — that you weren't directly involved in the fight. But you definitely saw the attackers, and maybe you even know them. Or maybe the friend who was with you knows them."

I didn't know why he was stressing the difference between the knowledge of the local police and his own. Maybe he knows more, maybe less. Or was he just trying to emphasize that he didn't really belong there? But why was he questioning me then? Even babies don't fall for friendly talk anymore.

I put out my cigarette and got another one straight away.

I didn't want to decline the cigarette even though I was beginning to feel sick at the taste of tobacco by now. Probably a new torture technique. Like smoking meat.

He was silent. I felt it was time for my little story. They wouldn't believe it, but at least they wouldn't be able to accuse me of not being sociable.

"It was like this. . . ."

I started slowly in case he wanted to interrupt me.

He was listening to me and his thoughts didn't seem to wander.

"I was walking home. It's faster going by the tracks. A train stood on my left. Somebody I don't know, who looked like a worker from the south, was walking in front of me. I was walking a meter behind him. Why didn't I overtake him? I don't know, I just didn't. Three men came off the train and started pissing. Twenty meters ahead a policeman passed me, running in the opposite direction. Past the man in front and me. Towards those other three men. I looked back and saw him shouting at them. By this time I'd come to the dried-up larch. A path turns off there and you get onto the road through a hole in the fence. From there I could no longer see what was going on at the flyover. And that's all."

He didn't say anything. A poor story.

The truth is a matter of taste. And I, as its author, didn't like that story. How bad must it have seemed to him?

We lit another cigarette. I was about to throw up.

"I've read your file," he added in a casual way.

Oh my old sins, go and stand proudly in line. Somewhere up there, there's always an angel who writes everything down, not missing one little thing.

He didn't start listing them. He took a few puffs and then added, more to himself than me, "As if I was reading the files of two different people."

He paused a little, and when he spoke again there was just a faint smile around his lips.

"A young man still searching for himself."

Was he cynical? It passed to quickly for me to decide.

A new pair of cigarettes was on its way. I understood less and less. What did he want from me? The only plausible explanation was a war of nerves. But I couldn't get rid of the feeling that it wasn't that. There was something else.

He leaned forward with a lighter. It was only then that I noticed a stitch on his epaulette. I couldn't stop my right arm from quickly moving to the epaulette on my jacket. He'd already sat back by now.

The seams were the same. There was no doubt. They'd

been sewn by the same hand. I stroked the seam and moved my hand away. I couldn't see even a twitch on his face.

We smoked in silence.

"I wanted to see you," he said and looked at his watch.

I got up. Hesitantly. I didn't know if the clichéd gesture, saying it's time to go, meant the same in this situation. In this room.

It did.

We shook hands and said goodbye.

I stepped out of the office. The policeman was waiting outside. He took me back behind the iron bars. I looked out at the foundry but didn't have a cigarette. My stomach couldn't bear even the thought of one.

So this was the fine gentleman in his prime who was currently visiting Karla.

The two policemen who'd brought me in with the Black Maria came for me. They were considerably friendlier. There was no shoving. I walked between them along the corridor. Through the door onto the pavement. We stopped.

They said nothing, turned on their heels, and went back in.

It took some time before I understood. I made the first steps at snail's pace, expecting at any moment to hear shouting from behind me. There was none.

I walked faster and faster towards the bar.

I still didn't know why they'd released me. Did I have Karla to thank for my freedom, or did they let me go just because they couldn't prove anything?

Now they have reason to lock me up every time I spit on the pavement or jaywalk. At night, on my way home, I often see the police in their patrol cars. Were they going to take me with them every time now? For a pleasant ride into the hills for a session of beating? I somehow didn't feel as light as a feather. It's a strange world. You don't like it when imprisoned or when free.

The bar was empty. I wasn't in the mood for being alone.

I didn't want to go to Karla's either. First, I had to make sure she really was involved.

I went to Magda's. It was time for lunch.

She opened the door, and a nice smell wafted out from the kitchen. She didn't fall into my arms.

I wanted to put my arms around her waist but she pushed me away. She was as cold as ice.

"Come in," she said very inhospitably.

I followed her into the kitchen. I knew what I was in for. Sometimes I am in the right mood for a kick up my ass, but this time I wasn't. I could've left straight away. I thought, though, it was only fair to listen to Magda's speech, which she had probably spent quite some time rehearsing, before we said goodbye.

She didn't ask me to sit down. We stood there with a safe distance of two meters between us.

"It's finished," she started. Classic. "I don't know what was the matter with me to have been so crazy about you. I've got a boyfriend now and I told him everything yesterday. We had a talk. Whatever it was that I was obsessed with, it's over now. Never again. Sometime I'll ask you what you felt for me. Not now but in a few years time. Goodbye, Egon."

I nodded and went to the door. Short and sweet. Not a bad speech.

I stepped across the threshold, pushing my head down between my shoulders, expecting a loud slam of the door. It wasn't that bad though.

The key turned twice, in quick succession.

I was in the street again. I felt lonely and sad.

Too many things for one morning. Karla's lover becoming a real person, the first one ever since I'd known her. Magda throwing me out. The police throwing me out.

I felt abandoned and unwanted by everybody.

I needed a walk. I dragged my index finger along the foundry fence, letting it vibrate.

I stopped in front of the nail packaging plant. I climbed

over the fence. I followed the conveyor belt to the end. Ajsha was stamping.

"Hey!" I shouted into her ear.

She looked up without stopping her hand.

"Hi."

"Egon, what are you doing here? You're too late for lunch."

"I'd like to ask you something. Are you coming to the dance tonight?"

"What?"

"THE DANCE!" I screamed.

Where did the whispered gentle invitations go? I bent closer to her ear and added, "It would mean a lot to me."

I looked at her pleadingly.

She thought for a long time. A terrible coquette. Her hand kept going *stamp, stamp, stamp, stamp.* At last she said, "Maybe."

I was overjoyed by her acceptance.

I waved to her and ran off.

I jumped over the fence, and in my ears I could still hear the noise of the nails falling.

I sat in the bar and didn't move until evening. The chairs were gradually getting taken. I bummed half a sandwich from some student. More and more acquaintances were sitting around me. The circles were becoming complete.

In the corner, Sheriff was brushing some fluff off his Stetson. The tension in the air was growing. The place was overflowing with people. They stood between the tables, shared chairs. Some sat on tables. Drink flowed in streams. Empty bottles were rolling among our feet. I was greeting people left, right and center and had difficulty keeping up with all the bottles that were offered to me. The heat of Friday night made everyone a lot more generous than usual.

The majority were workers from the foundry, the schoolboys and girls were in the minority.

Suddenly I realized I knew everybody by their significant

features, not their names. One of them could juggle with his cigarette, another one could eat glass. Or spit the farthest through his teeth. Or had cavities in his teeth that he could put pencils into. And felt tip pens in his wisdom teeth. One could belch the loudest. Another one could fart longest without interruption. Yet another one could drink the most slivovitz at once. Then followed a hierarchy according to strength, fighting ability, years in prison. There was somebody whose intellectual abilities were at the level of an idiot. But he could list all the footballers in all the leagues, even those from remote villages, and the scorers of all the goals at any match for the past twenty years, all the fouls, referees, and probably all the fans in the stands, even though I'd never actually asked him about those. His achievement was even more admirable because of his not being able to read or write. He learned all the details only from listening to people. But I suppose that's not so difficult as football is not exactly a rare subject of conversation in certain circles.

Everybody tried to stand out in his own way. According to their best abilities and means. To be different.

I was hoping the Hadžipuzić brothers would soon send me the Cartier.

Ibro pushed through the crowd. In a new suit and shoes. He'd fulfilled my expectations.

He'd bought a suede jacket and trousers with a fringe running from the shoulder down in horizontal lines with ten centimeter gaps between each line. On his feet, huge winkle-pickers with raised heels. Polished to a perfect shine.

He'd pinned a tin sheriff's badge to his chest. They were selling them at the toystore for children to play cowboys and Indians. His hat came from the same set. Made of cardboard, covered with shiny blue plastic.

He stepped towards Sheriff's table. He was looking around, obviously pleased with himself, judging by the smile on his face. I waved to him.

"How's Selim?" I tried to shout over the noise.

"He's all right! He was at work today!" He shouted back and then ordered me a beer.

A new wave of people coming in engulfed me.

Somebody said hello right next to my right ear. Selim.

He squatted next to my table. We looked each other in the eye. He was saying something. Quietly. I couldn't catch a word.

I felt terror creeping from my stomach up along my back. I jumped up and fought my way to the bathroom. I locked myself into a stall and leaned my head on the door.

I was getting an attack. The first one after quite a few years. I started shaking with fear. I bent over into a fetal position, sliding down onto the tiled floor. I was falling. Into fear. Into nothingness. I wasn't there anymore. I didn't exist. I was nowhere. In nonexistence.

A terrible feeling of horror pulled me out. Sobbing "no no no no no no," I jumped up and became aware of my surroundings. I stared at the shitty toilet until the terror went. I felt myself with my hands. I was wet.

Drowning in sweat. I put my head under the cold tap. It helped. I wiped my face in my jacket and joined the crowd.

I knew the attack was brought on by Selim's eyes. I remembered where I'd seen them before. They were my own eyes. When I'd straightened up and seen them in the mirror, before I . . . Shit! Oh God, was I really going to have to be present when somebody else went down the path I'd already been on?

"What do I look like?" shouted Ibro and pushed a beer in my hand.

I drank the whole bottle in one long gulp.

"Awesome," I admitted admiringly.

"Have you invited Ajsha?"

Only then I remembered my promise from the day before, well, half a promise really.

"I have."

Ibro wanted to kiss me. At the last moment a space appeared behind me, into which I retreated.

Another beer found its way into my hands.

"You're a real pal," he said, slapping me on my shoulder enthusiastically.

I noticed a plastic light blue belt covered with stars. The holster for the toy pistol was empty. Beneath it swayed three tassels.

LONESOME RIDER was written on it in gold letters.

"You'll see! Today is going to be a day like no other," Ibro half-sang prophetically.

Four big guys were pushing their way towards the exit and carried me with them. I stopped at the other side of the bar and finished the beer I'd been given. Selim was nowhere to be seen.

Two policemen were making their way through the crowd. Asking somebody for an identification card every half a meter. I turned the other way and stared at the ads and notices on the wall. I sneakily turned around to see if they'd gone past. We looked at each other. Twenty centimeters apart.

They didn't say anything. As if I wasn't there. They continued shoving their way to the bar to pester the waitress for giving alcohol to those under age.

Karla must have done something. I'd have to go and thank her tomorrow.

I made my way out. Had a piss against the wall of the bar.

The dance had already started. Music could be heard.

I set off for the school. It was only a hundred meters away.

Selim was standing on the corner. He was looking before him with the look of a man who'd already seen everything and could no longer be surprised by anything.

I went over to him and lit a cigarette.

"I'm waiting for Ibro," he said.

"Has he gone for a piss?"

I pointed to the bushes growing at the side of the building.

"No."

He sighed deeply.

"What's he doing then? Shitting?"

"He's putting perfume on."

He looked at me as if I were to blame. At least partly.

"Selim, I don't put mine on in the bushes. I don't quite understand what's going on."

"Ibro was listening to that ponytail in the bar, what do you call him?"

"Hippy."

"Yeah, that's the one. He was telling us that there's this species of frog, where the male's sperm madly arouses the female. Once they smell it, they run for kilometers to reach the male. He added that the scientists have observed the same in people."

He sighed again.

I started laughing. In a malicious, nasty sort of way.

"You're saying that Ibro is now in there all on his own," I pointed at the bushes, "anointing himself with his semen?"

"Yes," he said, "he's putting semen on himself."

"Where?"

"Behind his ears."

Selim didn't join in my laughter. He seemed exasperated with the stupidity of the world. I stopped laughing.

The branches of the bushes were moving rhythmically.

I took a last puff and flicked the cigarette high along the wall.

I sighed.

"You're right. I should really cry, not laugh. But even if it's true, there's a fundamental flaw in what he's doing. Once you're close enough for a girl to be able to sniff behind your ears, it doesn't matter anymore whether you've got spunk there or not. So."

"But he has bought some perfume as well."

"Oh yeah, which one?"

"The only one they had at the newsstand. There's a black cat on it, if I remember rightly."

We stopped talking and observed the crowd rolling towards the school.

The bass drummed monotonously.

Selim broke the silence.

"Do you think it'll break him?"

He was referring to Ibro. To the wild enthusiasm with which he was getting ready to seduce Ajsha. We both knew he didn't stand a chance.

"I don't know. He seems like a man who sees everything on the bright side. It'll be hard, that's for sure. If this doesn't fuck him up, nothing will."

"It would be for the best if she didn't come at all."

I remembered that I had invited her myself that morning. I started regretting it.

"Yes, it really would be for the best if Ajsha didn't come. But everybody sobers up. Sooner or later."

I looked at Selim sideways. These words could've referred to his love for Nastassja, too. But he didn't seem to get it.

I looked up. Over the rotten gutter into the sky. It was littered with stars. Not even the smallest fragment was missing from the moon. From the road, women could be heard laughing. It was Ajsha with two friends.

Selim slowly released his breath from his lungs.

They went in.

Ibro came laughing from the bushes.

"I've bought some perfume, too," he immediately let me know.

"Oh really, which one, show me it."

He showed me it. The bottle was still full. Maybe there was still time to talk him into leaving it like that.

"Has she come yet?"

We shrugged our shoulders and shook our heads.

"Come on, let's go inside. She's sure to be there."

We went in. Ibro in the middle. He was clicking his heels and held his elbows out with his thumbs tucked into his belt. His every step was accompanied by the quiet rustling of the fringe on his cowboy outfit, similar to the sound of brushes in a slow jazz blues number played by an orchestra in a sleepy bar. Just before the entrance, I slowed down and peeped behind his ears. His hair prevented me from seeing what I was looking for.

"What's the matter? Are you afraid to go in?" he asked me, full of confidence. The absolute boss. I hoped I wouldn't be the one to walk him home.

"Let's go," I said and put my hand on the door handle.

"Wait a moment."

He pulled the bottle of perfume out of his pocket, screwed off the top, and splashed it in his hair. There was a terrible smell of cheap chemistry.

He grabbed his jacket collar and pulled it away from his chest. Poured in the second third of the bottle. He used the rest for consecrating his armpits and between his legs. The empty bottle flew into the night.

"Now we can go in."

He opened the door.

The glass bottle rattled on the gravel.

We stepped inside. The corridor was full of desks. In the middle, by a narrow passage, stood a schoolboy collecting the entrance fee. We looked through him. Pushed in side by side. Moved the table and the doorman sitting on it. He didn't say anything. A clever boy.

We made our way through the corridor and into the gymnasium. We didn't go to the dance floor. We stood in what looked like the locker room, judging by the hooks on the wall and the mirrors. We watched the crowd through the door. Somewhere in the middle, it seemed, people were dancing. Or at least swaying rhythmically. Along all four walls there was an unbroken rectangle of people sitting on the exercise benches.

Among the constantly moving bodies crammed against each other, I noticed Ajsha sitting with her two friends.

"There she is. She's here," whimpered Ibro. His confidence had all but evaporated. He'd gone soft, and it seemed as if he would just melt onto the floor between us.

"What do I do now?"

He clung to me like a drowning man.

"Nothing. Ask her for a dance."

"Yes, I will. Just let me calm down."

He shuffled from one foot to another. He shook every now and again and he probably really would have calmed down. Eventually, sometime in the early morning. Alone in the gym.

"Well, go on."

I pushed him into the stream of people milling around the dance floor. Mainly men looking at women sitting on the benches. Like in a market. I followed Ibro. Pushing away the elbows and the backs, I made slow progress.

Near Ajsha, Selim joined us. I was staring at something in the middle until we went past her. I didn't want to see her. I didn't want to be Ibro's scapegoat.

He didn't ask her for a dance. Slowly we made a circle around the gym and jumped out of the crowd into the locker room.

I'd had enough of this joke. I went to the bathroom. There was a queue in front of the stall, so I had a smoke.

While looking at the stream of my piss I noticed three coins in the toilet. I zipped my fly. I couldn't tear my eyes away from the coins. I sang "Three Coins in a Fountain" loudly, from beginning to end. I stepped out of the stall and everybody moved respectfully to let me out into the corridor.

A man who sings like that is capable of anything.

Ibro was in the locker room. Selim wasn't there.

Ibro reported, "She's turned quite a few away already. She only danced one dance with somebody and then sat down again. She's waiting for me."

I nodded and swam into the stream again.

I saw Magda with her boyfriend among the dancers. She said hello. I said hello. That's all that was left.

I stopped by the storeroom where they kept exercise mats. I lit a cigarette and looked through the glass door into the little room where they'd put the amplifiers and the rest of the equipment. Three schoolboys sat next to a cassette player, drinking wine from a bottle.

Somebody bumped into me. I turned around and exchanged looks with a boy in a black leather jacket. His chest covered in badges.

"Fuck off," he hissed.

I stuck my tongue out at him.

There wasn't enough room for a blow. Or at least that's what I was counting on. He kicked and missed. The hobnailed boot hit the wall.

I looked around to see how all that space could suddenly have appeared. I was standing in the middle of a semi-circle of his buddies. The local punks. Young boys, most of them around fifteen. I knew them by sight only.

"Egon!" The shout came from my left.

We fell into each other's arms. The leader of the group. We held each other's shoulders, cursing each other's mothers.

"Have you got a band?" he asked.

I shook my head and we unearthed a memory or two. The boys were whispering in each other's ears, and their fists returned to their normal position.

They looked at me respectfully. Punky and I were old friends. We'd often been beaten up together. The worst beating came once when our band went to play in some godforsaken village. I'd been talking to Hippy before leaving. He too used to have a band, and years earlier they'd been to play in the same village, with their long hair and beards. The local short-haired young peasants went mad when they saw them. They beat the shit out of them.

And then, years later, we went. With crew cuts, dressed in leather. The long-haired young peasants went mad when they saw us. They beat the shit out of us.

And so another small circle in time was completed.

Suddenly Ibro made his way through the circle. He wasn't paying any attention to whose feet he stepped on or who he pushed away. He fell onto me.

"Egon, help me!" he said in a croaky voice.

The punks looked at each other, trying not to laugh.

The neck of a bottle was sticking out of Punky's jacket pocket. I gestured to him. He gave me the bottle. It was schnapps.

I offered it to Ibro. He drank a third of it in one gulp. I gave the bottle back to its owner. Ibro was gasping for air.

"Are you all right?"

He nodded.

"Now I can do it. Just one more thing. Have a look, is it straight?"

The top two buttons on his jacket were undone. He was pointing to the thick hair on his chest, which was bursting out of the jacket.

"Is what straight?" I asked.

"This, for fuck's sake."

He kept pointing to his chest. To where his neck joined the rest of his body. I leaned forward, straining my eyes.

"I can't see anything. Do you mean the jacket?"

"No Egon, no. The hair. Can't you see? I bought it in Italy. It's like a sticker. You just put it on. They sell it by the meter." To show me what he meant, he pulled the hair away with his fingers. It really was stuck on. It came away like wallpaper.

"Now tell me, is it straight? I don't want to look like a fool."

"It's straight, Ibro, it's stuck in a perfectly straight line."

"Egon, I'm going now."

We shook hands.

"Good luck, Ibro."

He turned and took a step. I called him.

"What?"

I put my hand on his shoulder.

"Take care!"

He nodded. Pressed his lips together.

He went.

We broke into laughter. Everybody. I explained the situation quickly and we jumped onto the parallel bars by the wall. We didn't want to miss a second.

Ibro was making his way towards Ajsha, who'd just declined a dance. Both her friends were already dancing. He stepped in front of her and his body hid her from us. We stretched our necks. Ajsha got up and went to the exit.

Ibro stood there for another minute and then walked towards us. We waited for him in a tense silence.

We surrounded him.

"Well, what happened?" I asked.

"I couldn't get anything out of me. I was opening my mouth and not one word came out. Oh, God!!!" He sobbed. "Ooooh God!!!"

He went to Punky and took the bottle out of his pocket. There was about another half liter of the clear liquid in it. He put the bottle to his mouth and when he put it down again, it was empty. He stood there looking in the direction of his defeat. He let go of the bottle. It rattled on the floor.

He fell like a tree.

We picked him up and put him on the bench. We covered his face with a hat.

"I didn't know you could buy chest hair per meter," Punky broke the silence. We were looking at each other not knowing whether to start laughing or crying. The other boys were waiting to see what their boss would do.

"Where do you find them?" he shook his head in the end.

"Fuck it, remember where you and I met."

He grinned.

"Let's leave him in peace. Have you got that cassette of yours with you?"

"I have."

I always carry it with me when I go to a dance. It might come in handy one day.

"Shall we change the music?" I asked innocently.

Everybody was for it. The bass was still drumming. Over it a colorless women's choir was hooting.

We entered the storeroom, which was temporarily acting as a studio. The schoolboys raised their heads.

"Get out. You're not authorized to come in here," one of them said. He didn't make it sound like an order.

I took the cassette out of my pocket and gave it to Punky.

"Side A."

"Yeah, I do still remember."

He walked over to the cassette player and turned it off. He put my cassette in and started playing it from the beginning. A cacophony of whistling could be heard from the gym.

"What are you doing?" asked the schoolboy and grabbed Punky's upper arm.

He just punched the boy in the face without even turning around. The other two were dealt with by the boys. The cassette stopped.

The whistling in the gym got even louder.

Punky turned the cassette player on again. It started. We shook with the rhythm. A friend of the three boys lying on the floor looked in and opened his mouth for a question. He had it shut with a boot.

We were shouting the chorus at each other. Dancing on our vibrating toes. A group of workers from the foundry marched in.

"What sort of crap is this, you motherfuckers? Give us Madonna. Now! Do you hear?"

We did hear and we were surprised. Who did they want?

Punky started looking through the cassettes. He couldn't find Madonna. He gave the worker a kick in the groin. The man's friends didn't look very pleased. People started fighting left right and center. The punks drove the workers out of the room. Other people thought it was a fight based on nationality and joined in. I was making my way to the wall. The whole gym was one big fighting ring. Somebody launched at me. I kicked him in the balls with all my strength and ran away.

A few meters in front of the locker room I spotted Ajsha. She was holding hands with some good-looking guy. They were running in my direction.

Directly above me was a basketball hoop on a wooden board. I waited for a gap between the escaping bodies, jumped up, and grabbed hold of the hoop.

I swung. Mr. Handsome came nearer. I kicked forward, let go of the hoop, and hit his right cheek with my foot. He didn't offer me his left cheek. He folded like a tie into a bowl of soup.

A rattle and a squeak could be heard from above. The hoop fell down. I pushed Ajsha out of the way. The wooden boards shattered on the parquet floor. The hands of those fighting grabbed them immediately and struck at each other.

I took hold of her hand and pulled her towards me. I put my left arm around her and started making towards the exit. She followed me willingly. The locker room was a bottleneck between those running out and those eager to fight, storming in so as not to miss out. We were moving slowly, a few steps forward and then back again, depending on which side had more people taking part at each point. From the middle, I forced my way through to the wall and then started moving slowly along it, holding Ajsha's hand.

The bodies weren't so dense there; the worst fights were taking place in the middle.

A mirror covered the whole wall. From floor to ceiling. Boxer was sobbing with his face against the mirror.

"Out of my way! Let me out! What've I done to you? I want out! I've had enough of this meeting."

In his younger days he'd been an ardent functionary, the president of the youth organization. A mustached Komsomol. Sometimes the drink would take him back to the days of his youth. Like this time. I was surprised at the liveliness of those bygone meetings. For a moment I regretted never having taken part in one.

"Let me out!" He raised his voice. "I'm warning you for the last time, let me out. Otherwise I'm going to hit you!"

The reflection in the mirror was still trying to catch him. Boxer started to strike. But he had no real strength. His hands were soft due to drink. The mirror remained whole.

Whichever way he tried to maneuver, whichever punch he tried to use, he always hit his opponent's fist. He gave up. Leaned against his reflection and moaned. A bottle flew past my head and broke off the top of the mirror.

A diagonal crack appeared down to the floor.

I could see my image becoming distorted. The two halves were shaking. I let go of Ajsha's hand. I stood in front of the mirror, my left hand up in the air, my right hand on my heart. I started reciting, "Mirror crack'd from side to side . . ."

Ajsha looked at me with horror and incomprehension.

I mumbled over the forgotten line but finished the next one in full voice:

". . . the Lady of Shalott cried!"

A second bottle finally shattered the mirror. It broke into fragments and scattered on the floor.

Strange that they don't love Lord Tennyson around here. I turned to Ajsha, took her hand, and smiled encouragingly.

We squeezed into a corner and waited. The stream of those eager to fight was slowly subsiding. The direction of movement through the locker room changed slowly. Those running away were winning.

I looked into the gym. A magnificent, huge, megalomaniacal

fight. The other basketball hoop was shattered, too. In the corner on the left, four muscular guys were holding Ibro in their arms, swinging him and smashing his head against the wall. Selim stormed in from somewhere and started hitting them.

"Let's go!" I shouted to Ajsha and pulled her after me. We made our way to the exit along the wall where the glass fragments were on the floor. On the way I tapped Boxer on the shoulder, turned him the other way, and told him to run out. He went like a bulldozer. We sheltered behind him. In the middle of the corridor he lost his bearings and stormed into the bathrooms. We went forward. Wanting to get out of the building.

A siren could be heard from outside. The police came pouring in through the door. Wearing different uniforms than usual. With long batons. They were striking everywhere.

I pulled Ajsha to the right, up the stairs. The passage was blocked by desks. We jumped over them and got to the top in the dark.

I listened to see if anybody was following us. I couldn't hear anybody.

They must've been too busy downstairs.

I pushed a small steel door, and we found ourselves in the attic. Full of old junk. Broken desks, placards, and decorations from various festivals.

I sat on a desk. Wiped the dust off for Ajsha. I offered her a cigarette.

We smoked slowly.

After the third puff, a barrage of words came pouring from her. About the madmen and maniacs surrounding us. I interrupted her and asked if she remembered the scarecrow in a cowboy outfit who'd asked her for a dance.

"Of course. He was the worst. I was looking at the floor and suddenly a pair of winkle-pickers appeared in front of me. I didn't want to look up at all. I was waiting for him to go. He didn't. I looked at him, I can't remember anymore what he looked like, and I saw him staring at me opening his mouth. Like a fish. At first I thought that he had something stuck in his throat. Or that he was suffocating. Then I thought he was going to throw up. I ran away. What if he'd dirtied my one-month-old blouse or shoes. I bought them in Italy. I'd said to myself I had to wear something red. . . ."

I was looking around. The moonlight shone through a large round glassless window in the middle of the wall, making the room appear blue.

Ajsha suggested we leave.

There was no point. We had to wait. We'd fall straight into their hands. I couldn't get rid of the feeling that she was at the same time frightened of me and attracted to me.

I stepped towards the window and looked out. The grass and road in front of the building were littered with Black Marias. A few ambulances among them. One fire engine.

They were well trained, I had to give them that. A Black Maria would park its ass against the door. The policemen would throw in the participants of the dance. When it was full, it would drive away. And the next one would come to be loaded.

I made room for Ajsha. She leaned on the window ledge. I was leaning over her. Shoulder-length hair. Pushed behind the ear on the left side, falling free on the right. The white of her neck divided it into two.

Everybody downstairs made their way through the glass. With or without help. Ibro was carried out. They beat him longer than the others. His hat was nowhere to be seen, his left winkle-picker was missing, too.

Selim launched through the door and hit a policeman. The blue uniforms covered him completely.

I moved my eyes to the neck below me. The fine hairs at the edge of her scalp continued in a small triangle down her back.

I pursed my lips and put them on her neck. I teased the hairs with the tip of my tongue.

She trembled and pressed herself against me. I circled her hips with my hands. My open palms slowly traveled across the whole of her back up to the shoulders. She wasn't wearing a bra.

Over the edge of her ear with my tongue. A gentle, short nibble of her earlobe.

My palms slid down her arms. Our fingers intertwined tightly.

I bent in front of her and we kissed. I undid her buttons. I kissed her shoulders and continued down her back. My chin pushed the material away.

Her blouse fell on the floor.

I removed her camisole on the way back up. She turned around.

I took off my jacket and T-shirt. Slowly our bodies touched.

The music from the gym stopped. The police must have advanced to the middle.

I dropped to my knees. My tongue swirled around her navel. In the meantime, I undid her jeans. I pulled her panties down to the middle of her thighs with my teeth. It said LOVE on them. I kissed the two hearts next to the letters.

With my nose I ploughed my way through her pubic hair above the opening.

Pushed into it with my tongue. I could feel her wetness on my cheeks and chin. In my mouth a taste of her juices. A hint of urine.

I toyed with her clitoris. She grabbed my ears and squeezed them between her nails until they bled. Naughty boys deserve that.

I could hear her fast and deep breathing. The thumping of my heart. The occasional slam of the door on a Black Maria.

I took off my trousers and underpants. I lifted her by her

ass to just the right height. She wrapped her legs around my hips.

We fell over together on top of a huge red panel. Large polystyrene letters squeaked under our rhythmic motion. I pulled my prick out and continued with my fingers. I didn't want to come too soon.

I waited until she was just about to orgasm before I penetrated her deeply again. She bit into my thumb. Her body flexed and she surrendered with a long AAAAAAAAA. I pulled my prick out again and moved it lower down, between her thighs. She squeezed it firmly. I pushed a few more times and ejaculated onto the polystyrene.

We lay there embracing. My thumb traced the outline of her body. Up and down. Slowly. Gently.

Everything was quiet outside.

We got dressed and stood in each other's arms by the window, smoking. The grass and the road in front of the school were empty. Tire marks could be seen on the ground. Only those with very good eyesight would still be able to see the hedge.

We threw the stubs down. Went to the exit. I looked at the letters on the panel. It said VICTORY.

My cum winked at me.

On the ground floor, broken bottles were rolling around the floor, which was littered with various articles of clothing. Drops of blood everywhere, in some places whole puddles. The odd tooth here and there. Even a set of false teeth. A pair of broken glasses. The bathroom door had been taken off its hinges and smashed. I washed my face in the ice-cold water. There was no glass in any of the windows. The icy cold night breeze was blowing freely around the corridors.

Ajsha went to the door. It was locked. I led her to the gym by her hand.

The fragments of glass crunched beneath the soles of our

shoes. The room smelled of cigarette smoke and sweat. The light from the foundry spotlights shone through the windows.

We waded through the wreckage. Only the metal frame was sticking out of the wall where the basketball hoops used to be. All the wood paneling had been used in the fight. The pale bluish light gave the room an eerie feel.

"Let's get out. I'm scared," she said and pulled me by the hand.

"Would you dance with me?"

She looked at me with fear.

"A slow dance. Smoochy," I explained.

She looked into my eyes as if wondering whether I was completely mad or just slightly.

"They'll hear us in the flats behind the school and call the police."

I tried to calm her down with a smile.

I took a plank of wood and went to the entrance. On the right, by the arch separating the locker room from the gym, there was a light switch.

I kept hitting it until there were only two little wires left. I straightened them with a wooden stick. A centimeter apart and slightly forward.

Ajsha was watching me, not understanding what I was doing.

Holding hands, we walked back to the middle of the gym. I kissed her cheek and went to the room with the music equipment. Ibro's hat was lying on the floor, all crumpled. I threw it in the air. It flew badly.

My cassette was still in the cassette player. I turned it over. I switched off the loudspeakers and put on the earphones. Found the song I was looking for. The most disgusting sugary piece, useful for certain occasions.

That's how it is with these old hits. Each one of them has a girl associated with it. But this one didn't have one yet.

It was getting one now.

I turned on the speakers and the cassette player.

The violins screeched.

A castrated voice started singing.

I went to the gym. I could see the outline of Ajsha's figure in the light coming in through the windows.

HEAVENLY SHADES OF NIGHT ARE FALLING

I couldn't distinguish her face.

IT'S TWILIGHT TIME

We embraced.

OUT OF THE MIST YOUR FACE IS CALLING

I put my hands on her back and my cheek on her hair. We danced, sliding our feet on the floor. Pushing away the broken glass and wood.

IT'S TWILIGHT TIME

Descartes was wrong, badly wrong. You can exist even when you're not thinking. The warmth of another body next to yours. A scent in your nose.

DEEP IN THE DARK YOUR KISS WILL THRILL ME

I had my eyes closed.

IT'S TWILIGHT TIME

The song was finished. The sharp sound of the electric guitar moved our faces apart.

In the light in the corridor two figures could be seen standing in the doorway.

With hats on their heads and batons and pistols in their belts.

Ajsha trembled and squeezed my arm.

I didn't do anything. I hadn't quite come to yet.

We looked at each other without moving. Only seeing each other's silhouettes.

Then the one on the right moved.

Rock'n'roll was blasting out of the speakers.

He wanted to switch on the light. He reached for the switch with his hand and started to shake. The light in the corridor went off.

A fuse blew.

Lennon was shouting, "SHAKE IT UP BABY, NOW!"

The other policeman touched his colleague and joined him.

A little choir in the background repeated, "OOOOOOOOOOOOOOOO YOU TWIST SO FINE!

The policemen were thrown to the floor.

I grabbed Ajsha, shouted "Let's run!" and ran, half dragging her behind me.

We jumped over the two men lying on the floor.

Through the locker room into the corridor. Only a few meters to the exit.

The door opened.

We stopped dead on the spot. A policeman.

A patrol car stood parked outside.

In the gym door, one of the other two appeared shouting, "Get them!"

The one just coming in moved. His eyes weren't used to the dark yet. We were already running. Left down the corridor. Two policemen behind us. The third one on his way from the gym.

On our right were the doors to the classrooms. We were far enough ahead to open one of them. If they were locked we were in deep shit.

By the poor light coming through the windows, it was very hard to choose the right one.

I grabbed a door handle.

The next-to-last door.

It opened.

Across the classroom to the window. I held Ajsha under her arms and pushed myself up. Landed on a desk. Turned around in the air. Then with my back through the glass.

Pressing her head onto my chest.

We flew onto the hedge. Bounced onto the gravel.

A policeman was climbing through the window shouting, "Catch them!"

It was meant for the fourth policeman, who was climbing out of the car.

We ran along the wall. Steps behind us.

All along the hedge. Through the dark.

Between the blocks of flats. Ajsha wanted to go to the first one. I pulled her onwards. The main doors were locked at that time of night.

One of the buildings had a broken lock, which could be unlocked with any key, regardless of its shape.

I pulled a key out of my pocket. Felt for the lock in the dark and unlocked it. We rushed up the stairs. There was a click behind us.

We waited but they didn't come.

We smoked, trembling with cold. Soaked through and through, we clung to each other. I put my jacket around her shoulders.

We smoked all the cigarettes right to the end.

From the windows in the roof, daylight started creeping in. Alarm clocks could be heard from the flats.

"My father will kill me," Ajsha moaned.

I walked her home. All the way across the town. She didn't let me go to their door. Just to the entrance of the block.

I removed a glass fragment from her hair.

The foundry siren went off.

She ran up the stairs. Looked back. She was too scared to smile.

I pressed my forehead on the glass.

My sweaty hair left a greasy mark.

I drew a line with my finger, cutting it in two.

CHAPTER 8

"I feel a bit queasy," said Ibro, putting his hands on his bandaged head. "I drank too much yesterday."

He dropped his hands back on the table again. He moaned with every move.

His bruised eyes were watching me.

He took a sip out of the bottle. Then moaned.

The waitress switched on the lights. The bar was full of bandaged heads and limbs in plaster. Hippy was dozing at the next table.

"I made a fool of myself yesterday. A complete fool." He tried to move a bit but gave up immediately. "I couldn't say a word. It's all right for you, you can certainly use your tongue."

I remembered the tickly feeling on my tongue from the hair on Ajsha's neck.

I mumbled, "Yeah . . . yeah . . ."

I sipped the beer.

We sat there silently. He sighed deeply.

"I'm not really suitable for her. I'd already said that. It had to end this way."

He was depressed. But not as much as I would've expected. It was the oh-fuck-it-it-can't-be-helped sort of depression.

I looked at him with admiration. Nothing can really depress his sort of character. He'd be safe till the day he died.

"How's Selim? Have you seen him?"

"He was at the doctor's with me. For the sick-leave note. After that he disappeared."

The foundry was operating with only half the workforce that day. The other half were on sick leave. They were sitting in the overcrowded bar. They didn't even feel like talking. Occasionally somebody would moan loudly. But mostly there was an unusual peace. The pensioners were laughing spitefully.

"I'm going to bed," Ibro said and got up slowly, stumbled, and screwed up his face in pain.

We said goodbye. He staggered towards the exit and then disappeared around the corner. Hippy nudged me with his elbow.

"Are you coming with me? To the hills?"

I nodded.

On the plateau, which confined the foundry on the right side, there was a village. Sometimes we'd go to the bar there to get drunk.

The battered yellow Citroen 2CV took a long time to start. While Hippy was torturing the car engine, two policemen walked past. They looked at me and went on. I froze, even though the probability of having been recognized by our pursuers from the day before was very small. We were only shadows in the dark. I remembered that I still hadn't thanked Karla for her undoubted intervention the last time I was held at the police station. I had to do it soon. Tomorrow.

The car struggled up the winding road, stalling and groaning. The village started after the next bend. Hippy must have sniffed my money, otherwise he wouldn't have invited me with him. It was okay. I'm not cheap, unless I can't help it.

We put stones under the back wheels.

He pulled a tab of acid out of his pocket and offered it to me.

I said no.

"Take it! It's strong! From California."

I didn't take it, in spite of California, wherever that may be.

He shrugged his shoulders and swallowed it.

A bony, mustached landlord was dozing behind the bar. We sat down in a corner and ordered a drink.

Three farmers at the other end of the room stopped talking until they'd had a good look at us. They didn't like us.

Leaning on the wall, alone at his table, the village hippy was strumming his guitar.

He was there whenever I came. The guitar's make seemed to be Mercedes, unless he'd turned the sticker the wrong way around. He'd always play the same song. And sing quietly.

The Stones' "Satisfaction."

I amused myself by trying to calculate how many times he must have been dissatisfied. He'd been playing it for at least ten years. Every day. Thirty times, let's say. The number was huge.

Hippy was quietly mumbling along. He didn't try to strike up a conversation. His monologues about his travels around India were of no importance to me.

I ordered the second and third rounds at the same time. The landlord was the type of waiter who makes you feel guilty for disturbing him.

One of the three farmers went to the bathroom. He tripped over Hippy's leg, stretched out from under our table, then kicked it.

Hippy didn't react. The drug was working. Calmly he moved his leg a bit further under the table and picked up his glass.

Another farmer went to the toilet. On the way back he tripped again. He had to make a long detour to manage it.

"That's enough now! Apologize!"

He put his hands on his hips and spread his legs wide. Real genuine country style.

As soon as we walked into the bar I knew there'd be a fight. I was resigned to my fate. There are things you cannot escape. They come after you. Earlier, down in the valley, we were the only two without bandages. The day after, we'd all be the same.

Hippy was looking through the man. He was somewhere else.

I got up, stood to attention, and started singing. "*Bandera Rosa*," an old Italian fighting song. Not with enthusiasm, more with sadness.

Hippy joined me. We put our arms around each other for support and sang.

The farmer got reinforcements. All three stood in front of us, watching us with astonishment. I was waiting for them to get fed up with the singing, to strike.

I didn't know all the words. I filled the missing bits with "*No nos moveran.*"

Hippy thought we were changing the tune. He didn't quite catch what I was singing. He started droning a different song, another Spanish one. "*No Pasaran.*"

If we were destined to fall, at least we'd fall with a song. A revolutionary one, if possible.

Those who didn't know the words could sing *la la la*. The dumb ones should at least open their mouths to prove our unity.

I wasn't looking at them. I was gazing past them, at the window.

Suddenly I thought I could see a familiar profile outside.

I shouted loudly. It sounded like thunder.

"Who says Nastassja is a whore?!!!"

The three men looked at each other.

"Whoooooorrre," Hippy sang gently, still in the Spanish mood.

The door crashed into the wall.

Selim filled the doorframe.

It was him I'd seen.

My resignation to my fate disappeared. I was filled with fighting spirit.

"Smash their faces!!!" I shouted.

The three men launched themselves at Hippy and me. Unwillingly, we found ourselves in the back line of resistance. It was Selim who formed the front line.

Hippy, leaning on the table, was waving a bottle around. Struck whoever happened to get in its way. Under his blows I was forced to move forward. Immediately I got hit in the nose. I collapsed and, sitting on the floor, looked at the blood running through my fingers. Faint circles were floating in front of my eyes. Somebody stood on me. I looked up but could only distinguish the outlines of bodies shoving each other. And the whiteness of the bandage wrapped around Selim's forehead.

I crawled into a corner.

Hippy still held his position. His bottle whistled in the air, drawing a semi-circle in front of him. One of the attackers ran up, let the bottle fly past him, then kicked Hippy with all his strength, aiming at his leg.

He missed and kicked the table leg, breaking his toes. The table slid to the wall. Hippy's body, which was now without any support, folded onto the floor.

His attacker was rolling on the floor roaring with pain. I got up, ran, and landed on his stomach. Fell straight on top of Hippy.

The man I'd jumped on was throwing up.

The other two picked him up and ran off.

The village hippy was strumming "Satisfaction" again. The landlord was looking at us with animosity.

Hippy, on the floor, waved and roared with enthusiasm for a bit longer.

When he'd calmed down we left.

Selim wiped the blood off his knuckles on the grass. Hippy climbed into the car and started it. He opened the other doors for us. His eyes were like ping-pong balls.

I refused to get in. I preferred to walk. Selim didn't want to get in the car, either.

Hippy drove off, wobbling above the precipice.

We turned off the road onto a shortcut through the woods. Just in case the losers come back with reinforcements.

We got lost even before our eyes could get used to the moonlight. It didn't matter. What mattered was that we went down all the way. We kept tripping over tree roots. Trying to keep up with our legs, which were overtaking us.

The forest thinned into a small clearing. I lit a cigarette. Selim sat down. I felt the grass. It was wet. I sat there, feeling the dew creep into my ass.

Far below, the foundry lights shone like a long snake.

"I needed a walk," Selim said. "To think." It sounded like an introduction. I didn't say anything. Waited for him to go on. He was silent for a long time before he spoke again.

"Fucking hell, it's all very badly designed, very badly."

I looked at him with surprise. His bandage shone against the outline of his face. He'd realized it very late. At his age he should have realized that a long time ago.

"I don't believe in God. But I'll have to start, if I want to find the one responsible for fucking me up like this. I have no talent and no gift. No chance to pull myself out of this shit. I'm condemned to the foundry till the day I die. There are many like me, you'll say. I look at Ibro. He's happy with everything. Some others, too. Their only worry is football. They think I'm crazy because I can't recite the names of all the football players off the top of my head. Something's bothering me all the time. I think. I can't stop thinking. I want to get away. Out. Away from the foundry, away from myself. I've already worked in Germany."

I didn't know that.

"A factory just like the one here. The same shit. Better pay. That was the only difference."

He got up and started walking in small circles. His voice was very clear in the silence of the night.

I covered my cigarette with my palm and took a puff. I saw my palm tremble in the orange light.

"Sometimes it seems to me that I'm the only one at the foundry with any brains. Too little to get myself out of this shit and too much for what I am. Just enough to be dissatisfied. I'm loading the furnace and I can't see any sense in it. Any monkey could do it better."

Selim was in a late puberty stage. Without a shadow of a doubt. He was asking questions we all ask at a certain age. Then we forget them and become numb. Some of us with a bang, others just moaning.

"They say to me, you're a free man. Resign and fuck off. It's easy to be free with pockets full of money. If you can just go to Rome on a whim. Buy a plane ticket."

I started feeling cold and got up.

Selim had set off down the slope. I caught up with him. Walking one behind the other we got to a path.

Suddenly he stopped. I walked into him.

He turned around. His eyes burnt into me.

"I don't want to be like the others. I don't want to. To just die with nothing left. I don't want that."

His eyes sparkled in the night. They seemed to be on fire. I trembled.

There was nothing I could say to him. There are things everybody has to sort out for themselves.

I looked through the treetops. The sky was half hidden by the hill opposite. I remembered Noodle, leaning on the wall of his bunker. With little fragments of shit all around him.

Selim had already walked on. We got to the valley without saying anything else.

Dogs were barking.

Across the allotments and into the town. The flats were in darkness.

We stopped on the pavement.

Looked at each other.

Walked away in opposite directions.

I stopped and looked after him. The wide shoulders going farther and farther away.

Maybe he felt my look on his back. He turned around.

"Oh brain, oh brain, you cause me such pain!"

I don't know if he'd heard me. He turned his back to me.

The mesh of the foundry fence threw a shadow across him.

A crane whirred.

CHAPTER 9

The postman was putting letters in mailboxes. We said hello and exchanged a few polite sentences. No, I didn't intend to return to the post office. Maybe we'd have a drink another time. I was busy. He laughed meaningfully. Looked upstairs towards Karla's door. Nothing can be hidden from the postman.

I rang the bell. And again. She wasn't there.

The door at the opposite end of the corridor was opened by a gray-haired, plump old woman with a hairnet. She'd probably been waiting for me.

"She's gone," she said.

I went closer.

"You mean out?"

"She's gone for good."

I was expecting it. But these things still hurt, even when you've prepared yourself for them.

"When?"

"Early in the morning. I can't sleep, you know —"

"Yeah, and?" I hissed.

"Half an hour ago some men came with a van and loaded

everything from her flat. They said they were taking it to the dump. She'd only taken a small suitcase with her."

I put my hand on the fence and squeezed it. My knuckles turned white. I was just about to leave when the woman spoke again.

"She left a message for you."

She stopped talking and cleared her throat. Small tortures bring great joys.

"She said, I quote, 'The same place as the jacket.' That's all. Nothing else."

She looked at me questioningly, dying with curiosity.

I banged my fist against the electricity meter cupboard.

She jumped back. Ready to close the door.

The cupboard door opened with a creak.

Inside there was an envelope. Sealed with sticky tape. I tried to open it neatly. Lost my patience and tore it open. A thick bundle of folded sheets. At the top there was a small sheet of paper that slipped between my fingers and fell to the floor.

I bent over to pick it up and read it as soon as I lifted it off the floor. It said GOODBYE.

Without a signature.

I opened the folded sheets. The old woman stepped forward. Hoping she'd manage to catch something.

I recognized my writing. In blue ballpoint pen. I didn't know this writing was in her possession. I'd searched for it desperately for a while. Later I calmed down, thinking it had got lost. That it didn't exist anymore, like most of the people from that time.

I lit the paper with a match, loosening the bundle to make it burn better.

The light went off. I didn't turn it on. I ran downstairs past the frightened woman. A ribbon of flame trailed behind me, illuminating the stairs.

The flame burned my hand. I threw the sheets over the

fence. The burning fragments slowly landed on the cellar floor.

I felt like a drink. I ordered five beers at the bar, arranged the bottles into the Olympic circles, and emptied them one after another.

I was missing Karla desperately. The stability of the world was gone.

Ajsha sat down opposite me and words started pouring out of her.

"My father won't let me go out until further notice. I can't go anywhere. I ran away from work. I wanted to see you. How are you?"

I gestured to the waitress for a new round. She brought five beers and a fruit juice.

Ajsha's voice rang in my ears. Half the words escaped me. I wasn't answering her. It didn't bother her.

I leaned my head on my palm and watched her. Like a beautiful doll. A few spots on her cheek. Probably from the food at the foundry. Her mouth kept opening incessantly. Her teeth were showing, and sometimes her tongue.

Every change of subject was accompanied by a slap on my elbow. Once she nearly took my head off with her hand.

"I've got to do something with my figure. It's nearly time to go to the seaside. Do you think I should start bodybuilding? What do you think? I could do with some muscles. Would you like me to?"

Slap on my elbow. She thought I nodded my head in agreement.

"Oooooh holidays! I still write to all the guys I've been out with at the seaside. Well, occasionally. Last year I said to myself, this year there'll be nobody. I put on completely black sunglasses. I didn't want to see anybody. I lifted them just a little bit to look at my watch to see if it was time for lunch when I saw him. He was so good looking. Tall. With black hair curling behind his ears. Very muscular. You haven't got curly hair or muscles, but nevertheless. Well. I met him again in the evening. Walking along the seafront."

I spoke. My tongue went its own way. I could barely control it.

"He was playing a guitar. By the full moon."

She looked at me with surprise.

"How do you know?"

I emptied the bottle with one long gulp.

"I'd wanted to leave all my makeup at home. Then I spent the next two weeks putting it on just for him. We still write to each other occasionally, you know."

I groaned. Ooooooh Karla, where are you now? And Magda? The poet from that literary evening? The small army of girls?

My elbow received a new slap.

"I'm very unlucky. I always fall in love with gigolos. How is that possible? Only men like that fall for me and me for them. Don't you think bodybuilding might help me?"

I didn't think anything anymore. Nothing. I wanted to be alone. Listen to silence around me, interrupted only by the sound of the drink going down my throat. A little bit of peace. I couldn't take it any longer. Her voice echoed around my head as if it were made of tin. I felt sick. I had to get rid of her. Quickly. I spoke. With a nasty voice. Malicious. With my lips pressed together. I looked into her eyes for the first time since she sat down next to me. I knew where that depth came from. All the empty space behind.

"Hey, why are you telling me all this? I don't care. I fucked you. It was fine. Now fuck off. I don't want to see you anymore."

She shut up. At last. I knew I was making a mistake. That I'd regret it later.

Her eyes widened. Only then I noticed what beautiful eyebrows she had. She puckered her mouth.

"Do I have to tell you again? Fuck off!"

A tear came down her left cheek. Sparkled in the light coming through the window.

Ajsha got up slowly. Her eyes were foggy with tears.

Another tear ran down her cheek. More and more.

She ran towards the exit. I stared in front of me. With the corner of my eye I caught the last swing of the door.

I ordered another round.

Looked around.

The bar was full. In the corner was Sheriff with his gang. Boxer was dozing at his table.

I concentrated on the bottles. Ajsha's tear wouldn't disappear from my eyes. I could see it on Karla's face, on the beer bottle stickers.

I was ashamed. An action I would like to wipe out, but it was done and it would stay. There was no way back.

Noodle sat in front of me. It took me some time to recognize him. I could see the tear even on his cheek.

"A case of beer!" I shouted to the waitress.

I took all the money out of my pocket, rolled it into a ball, and threw it over the bar. The waitress brought a whole armful of bottles.

Noodle was saying something. We drank.

"Fuck this life!" he sighed.

Once more I realized in horror what I'd done to Ajsha. I howled, turned around and slammed my fists on the empty table next to ours.

I bent over and banged my forehead on the wood.

I opened my mouth and bit.

I could feel the tearing of the plywood between my teeth. I squeezed with all my strength. There was a creak. I could taste blood.

Somebody grabbed my shoulders and tried to pull me away. More and more hands were on me.

All I could see were belts and jeans. Sheriff and his friends.

They pulled the chair from under my ass and pulled. The table slid with me. Two of them went to hold it.

They pulled.

I hung in their arms.

They sat me on a chair. I spat out veneer, plywood, a tooth, and blood.

Sheriff bent over me.

I lurched forward wanting to bite into the table again. Somebody moved it away at the last moment.

They pressed me against the back of the chair. Sheriff hit me twice. From the left and the right. He bent over again and looked me in the eyes.

"What beautiful boots you have," I said.

In spite of the circumstances, he couldn't hide his pride. Snakeskin and silver spurs.

"Cowboys used to die in these," he explained.

"From shame," I added, "because they didn't have any other footwear."

I expected a blow. It didn't come.

He looked at me with contempt and grinned through his teeth.

"I can see you're all right again, Yankee."

He went to sit at his table. His cowboys followed.

I really was okay. I spat on the floor. Felt around with my tongue.

The tooth on the floor was from the top right. I expected it to be from the middle.

It was probably because of the carvings on the table.

Noodle had his left sleeve rolled up. He cut a narrow ribbon of skin from his arm. He pulled it away a bit, then held it in his teeth while slowly moving his head away and cutting along the stretched skin with the razor.

He spat the noodle onto the floor.

"Fuck this life," he said. He was looking for a strip of

undamaged skin for a new noodle. His whole arm was one big badly healed red wound.

I took a gulp. Used the first sip to wash my mouth.

Boxer woke up and saw Noodle. He looked as if he was going to be sick.

"I can't stand this! I can't!" He moaned, fell on the floor, and started crawling towards the exit. He used to go mountain climbing. He thought he was climbing a vertical wall. Looking for support for his hands and feet at every move, he slowly crawled forward. Under my table he sighed, "How steep it is!"

But he was still making good progress.

I picked up the full bottles from the table.

There were quite a few.

A heavy battle lay ahead.

I started.

CHAPTER 10

I kept waking up all night, having to either take a piss or throw up. Each time, I dozed off again, only to have another nightmare. The first ribbons of light were making their way through the windows when I finally went into a deep sleep. I woke up in the middle of the morning, very hung over and still under the influence of the nightmares. A long shower with plenty of scrubbing with soap didn't help. I brushed my teeth, spitting blood.

I went to the dentist. I inquired who worked where to make sure I queued in front of the right door. I had to wait a good hour before it was my turn. I sat in the chair and the female dentist bent over me. She had a mask over her mouth. And brown eyes.

I wanted to tell her to get the rest of my broken tooth out. I could feel with my tongue that there was still some left. But she didn't let me say a word.

She stuck a bent needle into the tooth on the other side. I jumped.

"It hurts," she established calmly. "We'll fill it. But this one has to come out. Nothing else can be done with it. It's cracked right down to the roots."

She poked around the gum where the tooth used to be and pulled out a small fragment of something. She held it in front of my eyes.

"Wood."

Another fact.

"Veneer," I mumbled.

She wasn't surprised.

She tapped my teeth a bit more and asked, "Does this hurt?"

I said no.

"Just those two then."

She started to get the drill ready.

The dental nurse came nearer. She whispered something about shopping, got permission, and left the surgery.

Before she left, she mixed the filling.

The dentist was watching me coldly, as if I were a fish she was just going to dissect.

"If you ever used your brain things like this wouldn't keep happening to you," she said.

I wanted to answer. But she stopped me by drilling.

"Spit."

I rinsed my mouth with water and spat it out.

"I bet, Egon," she said, "that it was over another woman."

"Yes," I admitted.

"You'd think you didn't have an iota of brain."

I remembered her first name. Finally. I'd been racking my brain for it for an hour in the waiting room.

"Lisa, do you really think people are rational beings?"

She pushed me back on the chair.

"You're certainly not."

The drill whirred. She blocked the cavity. Without a breather she went on to prepare an injection.

"I don't know why I'm trying so hard. You deserve to have

it pulled out without any anesthetic and the wound cleansed with molten iron. After what you did to me."

She stuck the needle into my gums. I danced on the chair.

"Wait ten minutes."

I wanted to go back to the waiting room, but she told me to wait there in the chair. I obeyed.

She leaned on the wall and watched me. She didn't take her mask off.

"Egon, you're a prick. I don't know what I saw in you."

I didn't say anything, thinking that maybe I'd made a mistake to come to her with my tooth.

She prepared another injection.

"Open."

Three more jabs.

"I really don't know why I'm doing this."

My lip and cheek started tingling. They swelled and seemed enormous to me.

I mumbled, "Did you get married after that?"

"Yes."

"Have you got any children?"

"Yes."

She wasn't chatty. I shut up and waited ten minutes.

She got the pliers.

She looked me in the eye and said, "I really don't know what's the matter with me. I'll get my colleague next door. He's the biggest expert in tooth pulling around here."

She went off and came back with an older guy, bald, with glasses. He looked like a Prussian officer. Huge.

He got the pliers, grabbed hold of the tooth, and pulled.

I didn't even have time to shit myself with fear, it came out so quickly.

The tooth lay in the spittoon.

The nurse came back.

"Shall I make another appointment?"

"No, he'll come. When he needs to."

The nurse looked at my health card and started to say something. Probably something about payment. Lisa shook her head. I put my health card into my pocket.

"Rinse the wound with chamomile tea," she said, business-like.

She started shaking her head again. I quickly went out before she could say that she really didn't know why she was doing all this.

While closing the door behind me I heard her voice.

"And try not to kiss anybody at least for a day if you can manage it."

Before I finally left I caught the nurse's surprised look.

Spitting blood, I walked slowly towards the bar. I looked at the pipes between the hot air stoves — Selim's favorite spot.

He was there. He called me.

I climbed over the fence and ran to his hiding place.

"Ibro's brothers have sent your perfume."

"Really? Where is it?"

"In our room."

His head wasn't bandaged anymore. An ugly scar ran across the middle of his forehead.

"Where's Ibro?"

I was burning with impatience.

"He went to work in the morning. After lunch he set off for the doctor's surgery. I don't know where he is now."

I looked at him pleadingly. "Come with me to get the perfume!"

"I can give you the keys."

"I don't want to rummage through somebody else's room on my own. Let's go together."

He nodded.

We let the guard go past, jumped over the fence, and ran towards the dormitory. Not because we were afraid of the wardens, but because of my impatience. This time we both climbed through the window.

"The most fucked up of the wardens is on duty. A real spy. He'd definitely report me if he found out that I was playing hooky. He doesn't do anything but listen for who's coming and going and what's going on in all the rooms."

We tiptoed to their door. He looked for the key and put it into the keyhole quietly. Opened the door. I peeped over his shoulder. Ibro stood in front of Nastassja's pictures, wearing his cowboy suit, masturbating. He heard a noise and looked back. He froze. His prick deflated in his hands in a split second.

Selim walked over to him slowly. Ibro's eyes widened in horror.

Selim started hitting. Slowly. Like a machine. Every blow could kill an ox, let alone Ibro.

He knocked him over. Bent over him and kept on hitting rhythmically.

Droplets of blood were spraying around the room.

A bone cracked.

He'll kill him, I grasped with sudden clarity. I jumped over to Selim and tried to pull him back. He didn't even notice me.

I ran to the door, wanting to call for help.

Ibro wasn't even moaning anymore.

I looked at the bloody mess that used to be a face.

I grabbed an empty bottle from the table. I held it in my raised hand trying to decide how hard I should hit. I didn't want to hurt Selim, just stop him.

Ibro was progressively changing into a jar of red jelly.

I hit.

It seemed that Selim didn't even feel the blow.

The second time I put all my strength into the blow.

Selim collapsed over the body on the floor.

I ran to the warden and shouted to him to get an ambulance.

"What, where?" he wanted to know. He asked question after question.

I was jumping up and down with impatience in front of the door of his office and finally told him to fuck off.

I ran back to the room.

Selim had disappeared.

Gurgling noises were coming from Ibro's throat.

I turned him onto his side and hit him between the shoulder blades. He threw up his lunch and the teeth that had been knocked out. The hair on his chest got unstuck and curled into a roll. I started sniffing the air. It stank of vomit and blood.

And sweat.

And something else.

Cartier.

I bent over and sniffed Ibro. He'd put on my perfume before having it off with Nastassja.

I looked on the table. The perfume was there. I put it in my pocket.

With the corner of my eye I noticed that Selim's wardrobe was open. The bottom drawer was pulled out.

I looked at it, wondering what it was that bothered me.

The bundle of letters was in there, and the documents.

The pistol.

Walther wasn't there.

I squeezed the box with the bullets. It was soft and gave in easily to the pressure.

Empty.

Shit! Ooooooooh shit!

I looked around in panic as if I was expecting Selim to be hidden somewhere in the room.

The corridor was empty.

I jumped out of the window.

Nobody anywhere.

A group of children came around the corner.

I ran towards the foundry but changed my mind. Back to the blocks of flats.

Selim was nowhere to be seen.

I stopped and listened.

I couldn't hear any shots.

Not yet.

The ambulance siren was getting closer and closer.

CHAPTER 11

I got up before the alarm clocks in the other flats went off, leaned on the basin, and had a close look at my face in the mirror. I looked as if I'd been trampled on. Large circles under my eyes.

I couldn't find Selim. He wasn't in any of the bars I looked in. Nobody had seen him. I assumed he'd escaped into the hills. If he was going to kill himself he must have done it by now. If he was going to kill others, he must have changed his mind after all this time. At least that was what I hoped. There was no news of a murder or a massacre.

I waited for Selim in front of the foundry. He didn't come. Sheriff told me Ibro was going to be in the hospital for at least a fortnight. Ibro hadn't told anybody who had beaten him up so badly.

I went to sit in the bar. There was nothing I could do. And I couldn't just sit there either. The sound of Selim's blows against Ibro reverberated in my head. Only now it sounded like a pneumatic drill. Mixed in with the music they'd played at the dance. And with the sound of the boxes of nails falling in front of Ajsha. The sound of stamping. The rhythm of the heart.

It was all the same shit. Boxer was asleep on a low, wide radiator. Around midday, two policemen took him with them. He winked sleepily. Didn't try to resist them. I nodded to him, but he didn't recognize me.

The siren announced the end of the day shift at the foundry. I went out onto the road. I'd had enough of sitting. It was the right day for departure. A cloudless sky.

The wind was twirling thin dust on the pavement.

I looked around the town during the only three minutes in the whole day when this town is busy. Children were leaving school, workers were leaving the factory.

I spotted Long Legs from quite far away. I made my way slowly through the crowd and walked directly in her path.

She noticed me. We stopped and played a little game, which of us was going to the left and which one to the right. We laughed. I opened my mouth, wanting to start a conversation.

Out of the corner of my eye I noticed Selim walking down the pavement. I looked at Long Legs with regret and pushed towards Selim.

We bumped into each other. He was deadly pale. The right corner of his mouth was twitching.

I felt a light poke in my stomach.

Something pointed.

The pistol.

"Take it," he said.

I took it and stuffed it in my pocket. I took the bullets from his left hand. I looked at the passersby. It seemed nobody had noticed anything.

Selim spoke slowly and wearily. As if he'd squeezed the last drop of his strength out of himself, then collapsed. As if it was the end of everything. When actions are finished, words want to have their turn, too.

The fucked-up body can't give them any energy or sharpness.

"I walked past the school. Earlier. All alone on the

pavement. With my right hand on the handle of the gun hidden in my pocket. The doors opened and suddenly children were all around me. My body just turned towards them of its own accord. I was pushing among them. They bounced off me like little balls. I held the heavy school door for a little girl. She was carrying a large drawing. An elephant in various shades of gray. Slowly I walked upstairs to the first floor. Children were sliding down the banister.

"Shouting. Or at least so it seemed to me. I didn't really hear them. No sound reached me. They were just opening their mouths. At the top of the stairs a girl was turning around and around trying to reach the other strap on her schoolbag. I helped her. She said something and went. I took the gun out of my pocket and shot twice into the bag on her back. A badge in the shape of a teddy bear shattered into small crystals. All without sound.

"Deadly silence. I went down the corridor towards the classrooms. I was completely empty. I felt nothing. A faint wondering why they were all running away from me and somewhere right at the bottom a feeling that this wasn't what I wanted. I couldn't stop myself. My body wasn't mine anymore.

"I registered a door opening on my right. I didn't even look there. Just pointed at it with my right hand and shot. Went on. A group of children escaped on my left. I didn't turn around. What was behind me was safe. A man in a blue coat jumped at me. He impaled himself on the barrel. I counted how many times I pulled the trigger. Once, twice, three times. On top of a locker there was a pair of small boots. Donald Duck was winking at me. I shot both the boots. Left and right. I registered a door closing. Pointed the gun at the wood. Pressed the trigger. It didn't do anything. I changed the cartridge. Walked at the same time. Dropped the empty one. Kicked it. Shot at it and missed. The window was half-covered with a curtain. A pair of shoes peeped out from under it. I pointed the gun about half a meter higher. Shot. Controlled the gun. The curtain waved. I looked at the hole in it. I noticed a small body falling through the glass and down. I stopped at the end of the corridor. I thought I could see a shadow through the frosted glass on the bathroom door. Two bullets. I didn't go to see whether I'd hit the target. I opened the door in front of me and went in. On the teacher's desk there was a model of the heart made of plaster and painted red. It burst. With another two bullets I shattered the skull on the skeleton in the display case. I went to the window and looked down. Waited.

"A police car drove up. An ambulance behind it. Three large blue vans. Their lights were flashing in silence. The feeling that this wasn't what I wanted was growing stronger. My body escaped. I had done something against my will that couldn't be undone. I couldn't go back anymore. Policemen in helmets and bulletproof vests were running into the school. I raised the gun and looked into the barrel. At first it was just a dark spot against the background of the members of the special unit, who were surrounding the building. I focused on the barrel and everything around it became foggy.

"No, this wasn't what I wanted. My body continued doing its own thing. My trigger finger bent. I wasn't there anymore. I didn't exist. NOTHING.

"NOTHING.

"NOTHING.

"Me NOTHING. An indescribable terror I'd never experienced before pulled me out of it. I found myself in the middle of the road. I was turned towards the school. Children were bumping into me. I was still holding the pistol in my pocket. The children weren't running away. They were playing catch. I tried to understand where I was. It was all just a dream. A vision. And suddenly I was filled with joy that I existed. It didn't matter where and how, what was important was that I was there at all. For as long as I can be. It's better to live, however shitty your life may be, than to have no life at all. The experience of nothingness is still pressing somewhere at the back of my head."

He stopped talking.

Those eyes were my eyes. Then in the mirror. Years ago. I wanted to put my hand on his shoulder and squeeze it. We had gone the same way. Selim, too, had finally and painfully arrived at what everybody knows.

Some of us just find it more difficult to grasp it than others.

He went.

Past me, down the road. Following the last of the line of workers.

I'd never noticed that he was hunchbacked. Or maybe he just held himself like that now.

He caught up with the workers and joined them. Became part of the crowd.

Disappeared.

I reached in my pocket for cigarettes. I felt the metal and moved my hand away as if I'd touched something slimy.

I ran.

Past the foundry, between the blocks of flats. The air smelled of food.

I crossed the tip, the rubble of deserted factory buildings. Through the ghetto, past the Gypsy settlement, I ran up by the river.

A forest came down the slope and let me into it. I tripped over a root and rolled down onto a narrow stretch of sand by the water. I picked myself up and sat down. Small waves were splashing against the soles of my tennis shoes.

I watched the weeping willows on the opposite bank. The branches reached down into the water that tried to carry them with it.

But they never went.

I put the pistol on my palm and looked at it. Something in its ugliness attracted me.

It was cold.

With a swing of my arm I threw it in the water. The barrel

stood up just across the middle of the river for a second. And then it was carried away by the current.

I took the cartridges. Swung my arm once more and created a few small splashes on the surface of the water. They disappeared even before I could count them.

I lit a cigarette.

From behind the treetops, which framed the sky, floated a dark cloud of red dust.

I didn't move until darkness came.

PART THREE

Now there comes a time to every man
When he must turn his back on the crowd
When the glare of the lights gets much too bright
And the music plays too loud
When a man must run from the deeds he has done
Recalling those days with a sigh.

— M. Heron, 1968

CHAPTER 12

The driver dropped me off in front of the foundry. It had changed in the fortnight since I'd last seen it.

I stood in front of the fence and watched. They were shooting a film.

They'd erected a wooden machine gun tower. Workers dressed in concentration camp uniforms were wandering around among the heaps of scrap metal.

The camera whirred.

An SS officer shot a sick woman in the head.

A guard walked past me dressed in a German uniform, with a helmet and a gun. He looked good.

I grinned at him.

He looked back at me with poisonous hatred and marched off onto the set. It must have made a good shot. He'd make a career in his old age. I noticed Sheriff in a row of prisoners. He'd replaced the Stetson with a striped cap. He was pretending he hadn't seen me. I waited for a break and called him over. He fiddled with the cap in front of his groin and hesitated. Without his boots and the cowboy suit, he felt naked and powerless. I understood that. I had been without my Cartier for a while, too. I didn't mean to torture him, just to inquire after Selim.

He hadn't seen him. He'd not been seen either at work or the dormitory for two weeks. Ibro was getting out of the hospital that day.

I said goodbye and left. He got back in line.

The bar was half empty. Ibro and Selim were sitting in the corner. Having a friendly chat. There really was nothing that Ibro would begrudge anybody.

He waved to me cheerfully. I nodded. I didn't sit down at their table.

Selim lowered his eyes. He was eager to get back to chatting about women and football.

I took my beer to the shelf along the wall. Above it there was a mirror that ran the length of the wall.

I watched their reflection. I couldn't tell them apart. They looked alike.

Just like everybody else in there.

I raised my glass and poured a drop into my mouth. Saw myself in the mirror. There was nothing different about me either. I could easily have joined them.

But I didn't go to sit with them. We all need to deceive ourselves, as well as others, if we want to survive. We all need a pose, a mask to hide behind. Without one, is it worth going on at all?

I left half the beer in the bottle. I turned towards the exit. In the middle of my move, Selim's and my eyes met for a moment. I opened my mouth, immediately changed my mind, and gave up.

If there is any emotional or physical state you're unable to express in three simple sentences it's better to give up. To leave it. To fuck off.

I went. After my legs, as they happen to grow out of my ass.

I stopped in front of the dormitory.

I slid the top off the dumpster. It stank.

I jumped onto the edge and dropped in. The real summer heat that had been around for just over a week had turned everything into a stinking, shapeless mess.

It squelched under the soles of my shoes.

There wasn't much garbage there. Just a few rotting bits of this and that.

I bent over and rummaged through old empty tins. Pieces of streaky bacon and onion peels between sheets of paper used in shops for wrapping slices of salami.

When my eyes got used to the dark, I saw it.

It was leaning on the back wall as if somebody had gently put it there.

A large photo of Nastassja's face.

I flicked a piece of rancid yellow bacon off her chin.

The other photographs were there, too. Both the posters. There was still a drop of Selim's blood on Tess.

They all went back to where I'd brought them from. They had done their work. I asked myself what was the matter with me, why didn't I just leave them there.

I didn't see any point in awakening the dead, but I still took the large photo with me.

Out.

I stayed sitting on the edge of the container with my legs dangling down.

My ankles and calves were splashed with the smelly muck. When I knocked my heels on the metal, the onion fell off, only two beans stayed on.

Long Legs came past in Bermuda shorts and a colorful T-shirt, holding hands with some hunk.

He looked like a model from a perfume ad.

The perfume I use.

He talked loudly, laughing at his own jokes. Long Legs was looking through him, watching me with a mixture of surprise and sadness, for which I couldn't find a reason.

They went past and at the end of the street, just before they turned the corner, she looked over her boyfriend's shoulder. I felt like running after her. But I just stayed sitting.

Without looking down, I straightened the photograph between my thighs. A warm breeze whirled the thin red dust around the deserted dormitories and rocked the plastic bags hanging from the windows. The foundry was wheezing, roaring, and whistling down the empty street.

I opened my palm, still staring in front of me.

I could feel the paper moving more and more strongly. The wind grabbed Nastassja and carried her with it, dragging her across the tarmac.

The photo was turning and folding. Dancing in the whirlwind.

Playfully it disappeared around the corner.

I sat there, and I didn't even feel like smoking.

I became painfully aware of the fact that the air around me was full of words and deeds, which had got trapped in between the hills and which ruled and suffocated the people, who were too weak to lead their own lives. The decency, morality, and conformity that make you normal.

I grinned and looked up.

The sun blinded me.

I raised my legs.

I rolled over and fell into the container.

I was already laughing while I fell. A loud but hollow laugh.

I lay there, letting the laughter echo around my skull.

When it finally disappeared, I thought it would be fitting to have at least a small moan. But I couldn't force myself that far.

I needed a moment to be away from it all and alone.

I didn't moan.

I didn't even think.

I just watched the rectangle of blue sky above me until it started to fade and grow darker.

It was within my reach but I still didn't strike and smash it with my fist.

Everybody must have something unattainable.